AFTER
THE
FIRE

A NOVELLA

BRANDAN
RITCHEY

HIDDEN
LAKES
PRESS

HIDDEN
LAKES
PRESS

Hidden Lakes Press
Lakeland, Florida 33813

First edition September 2021

For my wife, Dana

AFTER THE FIRE

CHAPTER ONE

His hands are rough — calloused. I've shaken hands with Mr. Peterson on several occasions, but for some reason, this is the first time I've noticed just how leathery they really are. I guess he has as good a reason as anyone to have hands like sandpaper. After all, he's been splitting and selling firewood longer than I've been alive.

"Building yourself a fire tonight?" Mr. Peterson asks with a subtle, old smile sprawling out across his lips.

"Yes sir, just a small one!" I reply. "Some friends and I are planning one last bonfire before our big summer trip."

I hand Mr. Peterson two crumpled up five-dollar bills and then bend over to pick up the large bundle of firewood from outside his barn. The words "Peterson Lumber" fill up the entire width of the band holding the wood together.

Kicking off the summer with another bonfire wouldn't have been my first choice, but the twins insisted and it's no use arguing with them once they get their mind set on something.

"Well, make sure you put out all the embers when you're finished, James. The last thing we need around here is another fire. You know as well as I do that this is one of the driest seasons we've had in years. Most places aren't even selling firewood right now."

"I know, I know. You sound just like my uncle. Don't worry, we'll be careful. I'll see you next time."

I walk toward the trunk of my 1999 Toyota Camry, the heavy load of lumber digging into the palms of my hands.

I open the trunk and pause, amazed by the supply of junk I've collected over the past several months. Old roller skates I've never used, a couple of broken tennis rackets, a sleeping bag that I don't even think belongs to me. Not sure how I'm going to fit all the firewood in my car, I begin rearranging what has turned into my own personal storage unit until I finally make enough room to squeeze in the freshly split wood. I close the trunk and walk around to the front of the car.

I turn on the engine and start to slowly pull away from Mr. Peterson's barn. It's an old barn. The wooden door is rotted out and most of the windows either have large cracks in them or are missing altogether, probably due to neighborhood kids who decided to play baseball a little too close to the Peterson property. I can't blame them though. Mr. Peterson has the largest field in all of Thomasville. When we were kids, the twins and I used to play baseball here almost every weekend.

I can't help but wonder about Mr. Peterson. Does he have any family? What does he do during the day? Chop firewood? Not exactly my idea of a thrilling life.

I pull out of the dusty, gravel lot when I notice the old, rusty sign hammered to the front of the barn. "Peterson Lumber" is painted in orange with a thick, red outline on a sky-blue sign. Beneath that, in much smaller text, reads "Established in 1955." The metal sign has little, pea-sized dents in several places, as if it had been shot with a pellet gun on several occasions. I give one last farewell wave to Mr. Peterson as I start on my way to Ward's Creek to meet up with the twins.

Sam and Scott have been best friends of mine for as long as I can remember. I first met the twins in second grade on the playground. A couple of the older kids at school thought it would be fun to corner the twins onto the large, red, merry-go-round and spin them around until they vomited. Well, there was obviously nothing "merry" about that. After a couple minutes of watching the event in frustration, I had the bright idea to swoop in and "save the day" like a superhero from some movie I had seen. It's funny. At that age, we seem to have the confidence to do just about anything. I felt certain that standing up for the twins on the playground that day would make me out to be a hero around the school. Kids from all grades would see me and say, "Look, it's *the* James Connor." Boy, was I wrong. All it did was paint a target on my own back for the next two years. But at least the three of us wore those targets together.

I check my GPS. Nine minutes away from Ward's Creek. I'm not exactly sure what's on the agenda for tonight. Sam and Scott mentioned something about s'mores and maybe taking a dip in the creek. "One last bonfire before the big trip." That's the way Sam described it.

We've been planning the trip for months. All three of us are starting college next fall, so we decided we needed one last "hurrah" before we get old and boring and busy with the challenges of what my aunt and uncle call "growing up." The plan as of now is to take Sam's car (a 2003 Ford Explorer) from Thomasville, Georgia all the way down to Daytona Beach, Florida. My aunt and uncle don't totally approve of the trip, but I think that deep down they remember what it's like to be eighteen.

I've been living with Uncle Ira and Aunt Terry since I was ten years old. They took me in after my parents were no longer fit to raise me. Some could argue that they were *never* fit to raise me. All I remember from my early life is hearing my mother break dishes in the kitchen while my father yelled unspeakable things at her in return. It was almost like they had their own special language — one I'm glad I never had to learn. Eventually, the neighbors caught on to what was happening and called DFCS. Before being put into the foster care system, my aunt and uncle stepped in and said they would take temporary custody of me, just until my parents could get their heads back on their shoulders. I guess they never did.

The sun is starting to go down as I drive over the narrow bridge on the way to Ward's Creek. I see dark smoke billowing up above the tree line. It must be the twins. The sun has completely set by the time I drive up to the campsite. I smile wide at the sight of Sam and Scott helplessly trying to build a fire out of "green," freshly cut branches, sap covering their hands. I can hardly see their faces through all the smoke.

"Looks like you're having a little trouble there!" I shout as I shut the front door of the Camry and start toward the trunk.

"We're trying to make-do with the little bit of wood we could find. Who would have known there wouldn't be any more firewood here?"

"I would have known!" I reply, lifting the heavy load of lumber from the trunk.

I slowly walk toward the fire (if you could call it that) trying my best not to trip over any large rocks or roots. As I finally near my friends, I hear them softly whisper something to one another. I couldn't quite make out what they said, but it was probably something along the lines of "Oh, someone thinks they're so smart." I don't mind. After all, I'm smarter than the two of them apparently.

"Why don't you guys try *this* wood? It should light up

right away. I'm going to go grab my gear." I walk toward the vehicle's backseat to grab my old, tattered, black, nylon backpack.

It's not that I don't enjoy camping with the twins — I do. It's just that, most of the time, the twins do what they want to do, simply because *they* want to do it. If I had mustered the courage to suggest spending the evening before the big trip going bowling or catching a movie, my proposal would've been met with a two-part-harmony of "Ah, man!" Or "C'mon, James!" Oh well. I guess that's what you get when your best friends are twins — always out-numbered.

"James, come make a s'more!" Sam yells out as I drudge my way carefully back to the fire. "We've got Starbursts, Twizzlers, and Skittles."

"For s'mores!? Scott, who on Earth ever taught you to make s'mores like that?"

"It was all I could find in the pantry. Besides, the melted Starbursts are actually pretty good," he explains with a silly grin plastered on his face. "It gives the s'mores a nice fruity twist."

I think about it for a second or two and then laugh.

"I think I'll just stick with marshmallows tonight, fellas, and leave the culinary experimentation up to you."

I walk over to the empty side of the fallen, rotted tree that the twins are sitting on and reach for the bag of melted-together marshmallows and try my best to detach one from the goop. Sam hands me a metal skewer from his camping pack and I begin roasting.

Roasting marshmallows was always one of my favorite things to do as a kid. I can recall several times growing up, sitting by a freshly lit fire made by Uncle Ira — a much more finely crafted fire than the one I'm sitting by tonight, I might add. I loved holding the white, fluffy, perfectly round ball of fluff over the fire, slowly rotating it so as not to char one side too much. On several occasions, Uncle Ira would fill our time around the fire with stories of dwarfs and wizards and dragons and caves, all the while Aunt Terry would be inside, baking a delicious apple pie or blueberry cobbler which would be ready for us when we finally made it back indoors. Tonight reminds me of one of those nights. Maybe it's the marshmallow (though, by the goopy look of this particular marshmallow, I doubt it). Or maybe it's just the fire, itself. The warmth it carries through the air. The beauty and life found in each flicker. In every spark.

The three of us sat there, eating marshmallows and Starbursts and Skittles for nearly two hours. Conversation filled the air. We talked about girls, summer jobs, what college might be like, and every now and then one of us would say something ridiculous which would make the other two of us laugh like idiots. Once, Sam made a joke that had me almost falling out of my camping chair at just the moment that Scott decided to take a heaping sip of his "manly, black coffee." The highlight of my night was seeing "manly, black coffee" spew from Scott's nose.

While our conversation seemed to dance from one

topic to another, there was one thing we talked about most — the big trip. We laid out all our plans to be sure we were all on the same page. I'm glad we did, because it didn't take long for us to discover that we all had different ideas about who would bring what and who was driving during which shift. However, by the end of the second hour around the fire, we had our "last hurrah trip" all planned out.

We talked a little longer and, while the twins seemed to have all the energy in the world, my energy began to dwindle along with the flame of the fire. My eyes got heavy, and my breathing did too. It wasn't long before I was sound asleep in my camping chair. That is, until I heard something that jolted me awake instantly — a loud "Bang!" that echoed through the forest.

CHAPTER TWO

My eyes fly open as soon as I hear the noise. It takes all of two seconds for me to discover the cause of my rude awakening. Hovering over the fire (which had grown significantly larger and livelier since I was last awake) are the twins, grinning ear to ear, their lips stained with marshmallow goo and Scott holding an opened, medium-sized box in his right hand. The box is bright yellow with a large, black, cat head in the center. Thanks to the glow of the fire, I can just make out the words "Black Cat Flashlight Crackers." I'm only awake for a measly ten seconds when Sam throws another firecracker into the fire.

"Hey! What's the big idea!?" I yell out in disapproval, my ears still ringing from the first one. "I was trying to sleep."

"We know that!" Scott admits, an annoying snicker plastered across his face. "That's why we cracked these bad boys open. Can't have you snoozing at a time like this. It's party time!"

"Party time? Scott, when was the last time you went to a party? We've been friends since second grade and the closest that I've ever seen either of you get to partying was in sixth grade when your mom invited me, Jordan Simmons, and Paul Randall over to your house to watch the Thanksgiving Day Parade."

"Ok, ok," Scott mutters, a little quieter and less enthusiastic now. "But you know what I mean. The three of us are celebrating tonight. One last night before the big trip. One last night to do something...explosive."

As Scott says the word "explosive," he takes his eyes off me and slowly turns his head, passing a subtle grin in the direction of Sam.

"Show him," Scott says, peering over his shoulder at his brother.

"You show him!" Sam insists. "It was your idea, after all."

"Ok, ok. Check this out."

Scott leaves his position at the fire and makes his way over to his worn out, blue and gray, Coleman camping chair. He bends down and picks up a large duffel bag from behind the chair and brings it over toward the fire. By the way he's carrying the bag, I can tell it must be heavy. He fiddles with the bag's zipper for a moment and then unzips the duffel all the way, revealing its contents.

"We are not using those," I immediately protest. "Do you have any idea how dry this season has been? We shouldn't even be having a fire in the woods to begin with. I had to go to three different places to find firewood for tonight. Plus, do you have any idea what Sheriff Burke would say if he caught me out here in the middle of the woods lighting off fireworks? Georgia won't let you shoot off fireworks at all, let alone during a drought like the one we're in."

"C'mon, James!" Scott whines. That seems to be his rebuttal to anything these days. "Look, we know your uncle and the Sheriff are friends, but you can't let that stop you from having fun. Heck, having the Sheriff in your pocket could actually help us have even more fun!"

"First of all, he's not in my pocket," I explain. "Second of all, because he and Uncle Ira are such good friends, if I ever get caught doing something illegal and dumb like this, you had better believe that he'll fine me twice the amount as anyone else just to teach me —"

Before I can even finish my sentence, Scott throws another firecracker in my direction and into the fire. I quickly plug my ears and leap out of my chair. Sometimes I wonder why I'm still friends with the twins.

"C'mon, Scott. Leave him alone," Sam demands, walking closer to the action.

That's right. I'm still friends with the twins because of Sam. Scott ruffles my feathers on a regular basis but Sam always has a way of balancing his brother out.

"If he doesn't want to light off fireworks, he doesn't have to. After all, he has a good point about the Sheriff, you know?"

"Thank you, Sam," I say, giving a little grin his way.

"Fine, I guess I'll go fire them off on my own while you two sit here sleeping all night," Scott blurts out, looking off in the distance with a my-feelings-are-hurt kind of expression on his face. Part of me wants to tell Scott to grow up, but I decide to bite my tongue.

He digs through his backpack for a moment, pulling out a shiny, metal, zippo lighter. Picking up the large duffel, he begins walking away from the fire in the direction of the dark woods.

"Where are you going to light them off?" I ask, half concerned about my friend's criminal record and half worried that he'll burn down the forest.

"I don't know. I guess somewhere out here," Scott replies, slowly walking further and further from the fire.

I suddenly find my conscience working overtime. My gut doesn't feel right about leaving Scott alone with a duffel bag full of explosives on one of the driest seasons in Thomasville history. After all, we're in the middle of a forest with dried out leaves and overhanging limbs and there isn't a clearing anywhere in sight. If I let Scott go into that forest alone, every school in Thomasville will be watching Smokey the Bear documentaries for the next three years. I desperately try biting my tongue — but I can't.

"Fine, I'll go with you," I finally mutter, hardly believing the words as they escape my mouth.

"Do you mean it!?" Scott shrieks, jogging over to my camping chair.

"Yeah, are you *sure* you mean it?" his brother asks, a skeptical and weary look in his eye.

"I do," I reply. "But, on one condition. I get to pick *where* we light them off."

"Where?" They both ask unanimously.

I'm not quite ready for the question at the moment they ask it, but I can't let them know that. The gears in my brain turn quickly, thinking about the type of place that would give us the least chance of starting a wildfire. It needs to be somewhere with zero overhanging limbs and branches. Somewhere totally clear. Somewhere with large open space. Suddenly, the perfect place comes to mind, but I don't let the twins in on the idea quite yet. After all that they've put me through tonight, the sight of them wringing their hands in anticipation is fairly rewarding. I decide not to share *where* we're going just yet, but I do explain to the twins that it isn't here and that we'll need to clean up camp and put our fire out before moving to our next location.

I jog over to the trunk of the Camry to retrieve the dinged-up, large camping pan to fill with water by the nearby creek to put out our fire. By the time I grab it and start to head back over to the fire, I'm greeted by clouds of putrid-smelling smoke. I shouldn't be surprised. It's just like the twins to mark their territory by peeing on a fire. I don't mind the childishness of the situation as much as the smell. The cloud of unbearable smoke lifts its way above the tree line. As I watch it slowly rise higher into the sky, I notice the stars. A completely clear night.

While the twins' urine extinguished our fire almost completely, I still decide to jog down to the creek to fetch a pan of water. In a dry season like this one, I don't plan on taking any chances. I roll up the pant legs of my jeans and take my shoes and socks off before heading too close to the creek. The last time I came this close to the creek at night, I mistook a wobbly rock for a sturdy one and fell all the way in. You can imagine how wet and miserable the drive home was.

I fill up the dinged-up camping pan with water and head back up to the campsite. By the time I climb up the small hill by the creek, the twins have abandoned the campsite and are already loitering by the cars, ready to go. I pour the cold, creek water over the remaining embers of the fire and hear them hiss and sizzle in response. After pouring the water, I decide to dump a little nearby dirt on the fire as well, just in case. I start toward the cars, picking up our remaining trash along the way.

I instruct the twins to follow me, still deciding to keep our location a secret until we arrive.

It's about nine minutes later when we arrive at our destination - the Peterson property.

CHAPTER THREE

Before getting too close, I turn my headlights off, bring the Camry to a gentle halt and jog toward the twins to give instructions.

"Turn your headlights off and leave them off," I instruct. "Mr. Peterson lives in a small house about a mile down the road. We can't get too close to the front of the property or we'll wake him up, but we should be safe on this side of the field, near the barn."

Sam, who happens to be driving the Explorer, nods and turns the headlights off. I get back in my car and lead the twins onward in the dark. I've been to the Peterson property many times and am fairly confident where I'm going. After all, it's a beautiful, clear night and the moon's glow is shining enough light to help me navigate.

It isn't long before I find myself driving by the tacky, orange and red "Peterson Lumber" sign for the second time today. We slowly pull our vehicles to the backside of the barn and park. I look up at the bright stars in the clear sky and smell the fresh air.

"Mr. Peterson's place, eh?" Sam inquires as soon he gets out of the car, making his way over to me.

"Well, don't you feel better about shooting fireworks off in a wide-open field like this one, rather than back there in the forest?"

"I suppose," Sam responds, a look of understanding returning to his face.

Scott takes a little longer getting out of the car. I see him walk in our direction, carrying the large duffel bag full of fireworks with both hands.

"Alright, boys!" He says, a childish grin spread thickly on his face. "Who's ready to get this party started?"

It isn't long after lighting off our first few fireworks that I realize just how little about fireworks I actually knew. I had no idea there were so many different kinds, but apparently Scott did — and he must have had every single kind of firework known to man in that duffel bag of his. We started off with smoke bombs, which, to be honest, were a little anticlimactic in the dark of night. After that, we broke out the Roman Candles and had what Scott and Sam referred to as a "Roman Duel." Essentially, two people would duel by standing back-to-back, about five yards apart. The objective was to aim your Roman Candle behind you in the direction of where you thought the other person was in hopes of hitting them with the fiery ball. The other person can move as much as they like, so hitting one another is actually a lot harder than you'd think. We each took turns dueling against one another, and the only "hit" of the night was when I managed to aim my Roman candle directly at Sam's right calf. He compared the pain of the hit to a light "pinch," but I think he was just trying to sound tough. After all, it's fire.

From there, we moved on to Bottle Rockets, Missiles, and eventually what Scott called a "Fountain" firework. This was by far one of the more impressive of the fireworks we'd lit off. Beautiful colors of fire filled the sky in front of us, sparks leaping at least twelve feet into the air. Thirty minutes must have gone by before I realized something that surprised me — I was actually having a good time.

"I've got to be honest," I admit as another fountain show begins in front of us. "This is awesome."

"I knew you'd have a blast, James!" Scott announces with pride in his voice.

"You're right. I think I just needed to loosen up a little," I say, my voice more chipper and upbeat than it has been all evening.

"And now, the moment you've all been waiting for," Scott says in a deep, circus-announcer-like voice. He trots over to his almost-empty duffle bag and pulls out what appears to be one last, very large, firework.

"Wow!" I exclaim in amazement. "That thing's huge!

Is that another fountain?"

"Not exactly," He explains.

I look over to Sam, who simultaneously looks over to me, another worried look in his eye.

"Well, what is it?" I ask, growing a little more anxious.

"This," Scott begins, "is the Gatling Cannon. The guy I bought it from only had one left, but he told me it was the largest and most impressive aerial firework he had. Those fountains you like so much are child's play compared to this thing. Plus, it doesn't just shoot out one firework at a time, like other aerial cannons. Inside of this one firework are five different aerial displays."

"Scott, you know as well as I do that a firework this big is sure to wake up anyone and everyone nearby, including Mr. Peterson. He probably wouldn't be too thrilled to know that a couple of high-school seniors were shooting off fireworks behind his barn."

"First of all, we aren't high school seniors anymore," Scott reminds us. "And second of all, you're wrong. While this thing is massive, it's actually fairly quiet. I saw one like this on TV and it hardly made any noise at all."

There's a brief thirty seconds of complete silence. We all take turns looking at one another and then looking at the firework sitting there, still on the ground in front of us.

Sam is the first to speak up. "Look, if worse comes to worse, we can always shoot it off and then high tail it to our cars and get out of here, right?"

"Exactly!" Scott exclaims, proud that his brother

appears to be on board with the idea.

I finally agree and we decide to go for it. We find a spot behind the barn to position the box and clear away some of the nearby hay. I look up once again at the beautiful, clear night's sky, imagining how much more beautiful it will be with blue, red, and green fire shooting through it.

Sam and I plug our ears in anticipation and Scott trots gleefully over to the firework to light the fuse.

I'll never forget how long it seemed to take for that fuse to ignite. The bright spark of the lit fuse seemed to dance slowly toward the box for five minutes, though I know it must have only been ten seconds.

Sam turned to say something to me, but all I heard was "James, I—" before the sound of his voice was interrupted by the loudest sound I've heard in my entire life.

While the sound of the firework *is* ear shattering and must have surely woken up Mr. Peterson, it's also beautiful. The sparks and balls of fire dance with each star in the night sky before slowly descending back to earth. And just as the first burst of fire descends back toward the earth, another crackling shot fires off, followed by another magnificent display, this one even more stunning than the last. I'm only able to enjoy this second round for a brief moment before Sam grabs me by the arm.

"James, let's get out of here," he says. "I don't want to be around when Mr. Peterson finds out who's been lighting off fireworks behind his barn."

He has a point. We quickly jog toward our vehicles,

get in and take to the road. We're pulling away quickly as another "Bang!" echoes through the field, followed by one more dazzling display. I watch it through my rearview mirror in amazement. It's a shame we can't stay to see the huge firework finish, but I think it's for the best. After all, we don't want to get in any trouble with Sheriff Burke the night before the big trip.

The twins and I decide to get a soda at Edmund's Gas Stop before we all head home for the night.

Edmund's Gas Stop is one of the few places in Thomasville where you can still buy a can of soda for only fifty cents. It's a two-minute drive from the Peterson property and has been one of our favorite spots for years. Before we could all drive, the twins and I would often ride our bikes down Harbor Street, play baseball on Mr. Peterson's field, swing by Edmund's Gas Stop for a soda, and then ride all the way home. Sam used to call Edmund's *The Watering Hole*.

We pull into the dimly lit, abandoned parking lot. The store is closed, which is fine, since the fifty-cent drink machine is outside. After pulling in, we walk over to the drink machine as we have so many times before. I don't remember the machine being in such bad shape. Its edges are lined with rust and dirt and dust, and the print on the machine is so weathered that you can hardly even make out what the drink options are. It's a good thing we have the buttons memorized. In any case, we only ever get one type of soda from this particular machine. Button number three — RC Cola.

We all get our sodas and sit along the curb for what feels like an hour. We relive the old days and talk about all the times we'd ridden our bikes up and down Harbor Street to get here. There's one particular story that the twins always like bringing up in moments like this that has to do with me falling off my bike and into a thorn bush. I divert the conversation to another topic. After a few more minutes of laughing and sharing stories, we decide it's time to get back on the road and head home so we can have at least a few good hours of sleep before the trip in the morning. We begin walking over to our cars on the other side of the parking lot. That's when we see it — smoke. Massive clouds of dark smoke billowing up above the tree line. And it's coming from the direction of the Peterson property.

CHAPTER FOUR

Within a matter of seconds, the twins and I hop in our vehicles and are on our way to the property. My heart is beating inside my chest more violently than it ever has before and my grip on the steering wheel tightens as I run all of the scenarios through my brain. What if it isn't too bad? After all, it was only one firework. How much damage could one firework do? It's probably just a bale of hay that a few of the sparks must have landed on. My wishful thinking is instantly dismissed as my gaze rises once again in the direction of the dark clouds of smoke. This must be a massive fire.

We're back to the Peterson property in a matter of minutes and discover two things as soon as we roll onto the property. The first discovery is the monumental size of the fire in front of us. The barn. The entire barn. Enveloped in fire. Through the flames, I can just make out the old, dinged-up, tacky, metal sign on the front of the barn that reads "Peterson Lumber Company." After looking wide-eyed at the fiery monster in front of us, we make the second discovery of the night. We aren't alone.

About twenty yards from the fiery barn stands Mr. Peterson. To the right of him stands Sheriff Burke, holding three empty Roman Candle sticks in one hand, and what's left of our Gatling Cannon in the other.

My palms are drenched in sweat and my breathing turns shallow. I don't know what to do. What *can* I do? I think back to this morning when everything in life seemed normal. Just this afternoon, I was here, buying firewood for tonight. I'd do anything to go back in time.

The twins and I are careful to keep our headlights off as we slowly park our vehicles outside the fence of the Peterson property. After putting the Camry in park, I quietly open the door and creep in the direction of the twins' SUV.

"What are we going to do?" I ask as Sam slowly rolls down the driver's side window of the Ford Explorer.

"I don't—" he starts to answer before getting cut off by his brother.

"We're getting the heck out of here is what we're going to do!" Scott interjects.

"Scott, this is *our* fault!" I explain. "We did this. Don't you think we should admit to it? Think about Mr. Peterson.

He didn't ask for someone to burn down his barn. We can't just 'get the heck out of here.'"

"Maybe *you* can't," he starts. "But *we* can."

Scott reaches for the keys of the car from the passenger seat, but his brother catches his hand before he's able to turn the ignition.

"Scott, James has a point. This is *our* fault," Sam explains as he pushes his brother's hand away from the ignition.

Scott looks infuriated. I've never seen my friend act this way after all the years I've known him. A part of me wonders if I ever truly got to know the *real* Scott Clements.

"Alright boys," he says, crossing his arms and taking turns looking at both Sam and me. "We burnt down an old man's barn. If we get caught here, Sheriff Burke is either going to lock us up in jail or make us pay for the barn. Do either of you have any idea how much a barn like that costs? Well, I don't, and I don't plan to find out. After all, he probably has his barn insured, right? If we leave right now, we'll be in the clear, he'll get his barn rebuilt, and everyone will be happy."

As I listen to Scott's argument, my mind wanders. Maybe he really *does* have his barn insured. Would it be wrong to "get the heck out of here?" My deep thinking comes to a complete stop with the loud sound of the twins' engine firing up. I look inside the vehicle and see that Scott was finally able to sneak past his brother and turn the car's engine on from the passenger seat.

For a moment, I think Sam must have turned the car's headlights on, but I quickly realize that the beam of light is coming from somewhere else. Sheriff Burke's flashlight is shining in our direction and he's walking our way. The twins see this and, after arguing amongst themselves for a short moment, Sam turns the car's headlights on, shoots a quick "I'm sorry" look in my direction and quickly drives off the Peterson property.

I find myself at an ethical crossroads. My car is only thirty feet away from me. I could make it to my car and get off the property just as quick as the twins did. But would that be wrong? Should I stay behind and tell Sheriff Burke and Mr. Peterson what had happened?

My mind shifts quickly to Uncle Ira and Aunt Terry. They would be mortified if they knew what had happened here tonight. They would never trust me again. I can't help but think about the time I had accidentally backed Aunt Terry's new car into a stop sign when I first got my driver's license. It was months before they would trust me enough to drive either of their cars again. Her car's bumper still has a grapefruit-sized dent to this day.

This is more serious than a small dent in a car. I burned down someone's barn. Someone's livelihood. I can just hear Uncle Ira's voice in my head now.

"You need to think before you act, son. What are you doing spending your time with those twins anyways? Haven't I told you they're no good for you?"

I don't think I could ever live down what happened

25

here tonight.

I decide to flee — fast. The light from Sheriff Burke's flashlight is getting brighter and more concentrated by the second. Thanks to the glow from the fire, I can just make out the silhouette of Sheriff Burke's stocky body approaching. Headed in the direction of my car, my walk turns into a jog. Keeping an eye in the direction of the Sheriff, I notice that his pace speeds up to match mine. I hear his footsteps growing louder as I race to the driver's side door of the Camry. As soon as I reach the door handle of the car, I hear something that stops me dead in my tracks.

"Freeze!" Sheriff Burke demands.

I see him now, standing only ten feet from me, shining his flashlight into my eyes with one hand, his other hand hovering over the gun in his holster. I've never felt more like a criminal in my entire life.

"Who's there!?" he shouts in my direction.

"James Connor," I reply quietly. I'm mortified.

"James Connor?" he asks. "As in Ira Connor's nephew?"

I nod slowly.

"Boy, you've got a lot of explaining to do."

CHAPTER FIVE

The walls of Sheriff Burke's office are lined with cheap, outdated wallpaper. From the peeling and discoloration, it looks as though they haven't been touched up in over thirty years. The desk in front of me is covered in colorful sticky notes, illegible scribbles on each one. I look up and see the large, cork bulletin board behind his desk, magazine and newspaper articles tacked strategically across it. Not one headline reads "Murder" or "Bank Robbery" like they do in the big cities.

As my eyes scan the headlines in front of me, I imagine a new story tacked onto the board. The headline reads "James Connor, Arsonist." My imagination is quickly interrupted by the sound of yelling coming from outside the office door. I've been alone in the Sheriff's office for twenty minutes or so, waiting for Sheriff Burke to return with Uncle Ira and Aunt Terry. I can tell that the voice on the other side of the door is Uncle Ira's.

"Randy, I'm telling you — this can't be his fault. He's a good kid! It's those twins, Randy. This had to have been their idea and they must have roped James into it!"

"Ira," Sheriff Burke starts. It's a little harder to hear the Sheriff's calm voice. I lean my head in the direction of the door in order to hear more clearly.

"The fact of the matter is that the boy burned down Chip's barn. Now, I've already asked James to identify who was in the other car that drove away from the Peterson property earlier tonight, but he refused to tell me."

"Well, he'll tell me," Uncle Ira explains. "He'll tell me right now."

I straighten up in my chair as soon as I hear the doorknob begin to turn. I look straight ahead so as not to make eye contact with anyone. Before I even realize she's there, Aunt Terry darts over to me and wraps her arms around my neck. Her eyes are bloodshot, and mascara is smeared across her face.

"Oh, James!" she shrieks. "Are you ok? You aren't hurt, are you?" She begins crying, her arms still around me.

"Yes, Aunt Terry. I'm ok," I respond.

I lock my eyes on one of the colorful sticky notes on Sheriff Burke's desk.

"James," Uncle Ira begins. "Randy filled us in on what happened tonight at the Peterson property."

I say nothing. A blanket of silence covers the room for what feels like an entire minute.

"James," He starts again, this time louder. "The Sheriff mentioned that you were involved in Chip's barn burning down tonight and we need some answers. I know that I raised you better than this. I know this wasn't your idea. Tell the Sheriff who was with you tonight, son."

Uncle Ira pauses a moment and then gently rests his hand on my shoulder. "Please, James."

Another moment of silence passes but is suddenly broken by Aunt Terry's emotional voice.

"James," she says, trying to hold back another wave of tears. "The Sheriff needs to know who was responsible for the fire tonight. Was it — the twins?"

I make eye contact with Aunt Terry for the first time.

"I knew it!" Uncle Ira shouts. "Those good for nothing Clements boys are no good for you, James. Why do you hang around with them? How many times have I told you not to get involved with those troublemakers?"

I clear my throat and muster enough courage to defend my friends.

"I didn't say it was them," I reply.

The room grows quiet again, followed by an eye roll from Uncle Ira and a sigh from Aunt Terry.

I look at the Sheriff for the first time since he walked in the room. His arms are blackened with soot, and he has large dark circles under his tired eyes.

"James, do you know what the penalty for something

29

like this is in the state of Georgia?"

"No." I quickly admit.

"A fine of $10,000 or up to a year in jail."

Aunt Terry bursts into tears and wraps her arms around my neck again.

"I don't have $10,000," I reply. My voice cracks as the words leave my dry mouth.

"Are you sure you don't know who was in the other car that drove away from Chip's place tonight?" Sheriff Burke asks, his voice now low and intimidating.

I think about it for a moment. I *could* tell Sheriff Burke, Aunt Terry, and Uncle Ira the truth. After all, the whole thing *was* Scott's idea. And the Clements family is far better off financially than Uncle Ira and Aunt Terry. I look back up to the newspaper clippings plastered to the bulletin board in front of me and imagine the twins' names in the fictitious headline rather than mine. It would ruin their reputation. But it could also ruin mine.

"I'm sure. I don't know who it was." As the words leave my mouth, I feel as though I made the right decision.

"I can save up the money," I say, looking Sheriff Burke square in the eye.

Sheriff Burke, now sitting in his office chair on the other side of the room smirks a little and looks in the direction of Uncle Ira.

"Well, to be honest with you good people," Sheriff Burke begins, "there hasn't been a charge made. Not yet anyways."

"What do you mean, Randy?" Asks Uncle Ira, his eyes wider than they've been all night.

"Well, Chip and I talked over the phone for a while tonight before you all showed up. He told me that the barn was insured and that all that was lost in the fire, aside from the barn itself, were some bales of hay and some personal items. He also told me that if James *was* the one who was responsible for the fire, he wouldn't press charges."

A huge sigh of relief comes from Aunt Terry who is still sitting next to me, now squeezing my hand.

"You mean there's no penalty?" I ask, breathing easier.

"I didn't say *that*," Sheriff Burke quickly replies. "While you wouldn't need to pay the $10,000 fine, there's still a penalty."

My eyes are glued to Sheriff Burke in anticipation.

"Come on, Randy. Tell us," Uncle Ira demands, his voice tense.

"Well, Chip said that if James was, in fact, responsible for the fire tonight, he wouldn't press charges. As long as —"

Sheriff Burke looks at Uncle Ira, then at Aunt Terry, then at me.

"As long as James spends the summer helping him rebuild the barn."

The Sheriff smirks and crosses his soot-covered arms.

"I hope you're good with a hammer, kid."

CHAPTER SIX

"Beep! Beep! Beep!"

I immediately hit the snooze button on the black, plastic alarm clock. I half open my eyes, just wide enough to check the time.

Six o'clock in the morning.

It's been three days since the incident on the Peterson property and today officially marks the first day of my "penalty." I'm supposed to meet Mr. Peterson at the barn, or at least what's left of it, at eight o'clock this morning.

I get out of bed and slowly pull open my bedroom window curtain only to find that the sun hasn't yet risen and it's still dark outside. I walk onto the cold, tile floor of the bathroom and grab my toothbrush from the counter below the mirror. As I begin brushing my teeth, my mind immediately darts to the fun that the twins must be having on the trip while I'm stuck here in Thomasville. My envy turns into anger. Not only did they decide to take the trip without me (the trip that happened to be my idea in the first place), but they also didn't admit to the fire being partly their fault. If you ask me, it's more than *partly* their fault anyways. The whole thing was Scott's idea in the first place. I'm just the one who got caught.

I shake my head and try hard not to think about Sam or Scott any longer.

By the time I trot down the stairs, Uncle Ira already has breakfast mostly cooked, and Aunt Terry is already setting plates at the table.

"I'm not hungry," I say in a low, unenthusiastic tone as I dart past the kitchen and toward the front door.

"Whoa, whoa, whoa. Hold it, champ!" Uncle Ira demands as he flips one of the eggs in the pan in front of him.

"No boy of mine is going anywhere until he's had a hearty breakfast. Now, take a seat," he says nodding in the direction of the dining room table.

I let out a sigh, but decide to give in. I walk toward the dining room table and take a seat next to Aunt Terry.

"James," she begins, a subtle grin appearing to her face. "I really think you'll enjoy today. Chip is such a nice man. And you never know, you might actually enjoy learning a thing or two about construction."

"I guess," I reply, not really wanting to talk any more

about the situation than I have to.

"Alright, who's hungry?" Uncle Ira asks as he walks over to the table with a platter of breakfast food.

Eggs, sausage, bacon, toast, biscuits. And it all smells so good.

Uncle Ira has been the designated Saturday breakfast cook in our family for as long as I can remember. Aunt Terry usually cooks during the week, but for some reason Saturday mornings in the kitchen have always belonged to Uncle Ira. I remember helping him with breakfast almost every weekend when I was a kid. We would find jazz music on the radio and pretend that we were gourmet chefs. When I first moved in with Uncle Ira and Aunt Terry, I was only ten years old, so Uncle Ira didn't trust me enough to actually *cook* anything. But he would let me crack the eggs into the bowl and whisk them up.

There isn't any jazz music playing this morning. Everyone is quiet, so much so that it's beginning to feel uncomfortable.

"So," Uncle Ira starts as he reaches toward the middle of the table for another biscuit. "Today's the first day, huh? How are you feeling?"

Although I don't really feel like talking about it, I do anyway.

"I feel ok," I reply softly, intentionally making eye contact with the jar of jelly on the table rather than with Uncle Ira.

"James," he starts. "Everyone makes mistakes. You're a

good kid. I know it. Your aunt knows it. Even Sheriff Burke knows it."

"What about Mr. Peterson?" I ask, still holding a staring contest with the jelly. "Does *he* know it?"

"Well, maybe not, son. But he will. Soon he'll know just the kind of young man you are. And you're going to get to know just the kind of man he is, too. I don't know if you know this or not, but your grandpa and Chip Peterson were actually pretty good friends in the old days."

"They were?" I ask, taking my eyes off the jelly and locking them on Uncle Ira. "I never knew that."

"Oh yeah," starts Uncle Ira again. "Your dad and I never got to know him all that well, but before your grandpa passed away, he and Mr. Peterson were fishing buddies. Chip has his own pond out there on the property where they would fish for hours."

I was surprised to hear Uncle Ira talk about Grandpa. He passed away when I was only two or three years old, so I never really got to know him. My entire life, every time I ever asked a question about Grandpa, everyone was always quick to change the subject.

"Well, he's expecting me at eight o'clock," I say, scooting my chair out from under the table and grabbing one last biscuit to-go.

"James," starts Aunt Terry as I'm already halfway out the door. "Behave yourself and try to learn a thing or two."

"I will!" I shout, shutting the door behind me.

The air outside is crisp. And warm. I trot over to the

Camry and start the trip toward Harbor Street and Mr. Peterson's barn. I can't help but wonder what the day will be like. I've never done much construction work. In fact, the last thing I tried to build was a fort in the woods with the twins when we were all twelve years old — and even that fell apart after a week or two.

Several minutes of driving pass until I finally pull onto the old dirt road that leads to Mr. Peterson's barn. I'm shocked by how different everything looks. The very spot where the barn once stood is now a totally bare area, appearing to have been dug out evenly about a foot deep in every direction. I immediately wonder how the charred wood, ashes, and rubble from the fire could be gone so quickly after only a few days. To the side of where the barn once was sits a pile of lumber, all different shapes and sizes. Next to the lumber pile are a few tables lined with saws and power tools. As I scan the property, my eyes suddenly shift to an old Chevy pickup. As I get closer to the front gate, I see Mr. Peterson behind the truck, rummaging through some supplies in the truck's bed. My heart rate speeds up as I pull onto the property, both nervous and terrified for what Mr. Peterson might say to me.

"Morning, James!" He says with a smile as I climb out of the Camry.

"Morning, Mr. Peterson," I say solemnly, keeping my head low.

Mr. Peterson turns back to the bed of his truck to continue rifling through what looks like large metal stakes.

Approaching the truck, I muster the courage to speak again. This time with the intention to officially apologize.

"Mr. Peterson," I say, trying to find the right words to say as they leave my mouth. "I… I'm really… I feel —"

"James," Mr. Peterson says, cutting me off before I have the chance to apologize. "I'm not interested in hearing an apology for what happened here the other night."

"You're not?" I ask, a look of confusion spread across my face.

"Of course not," he responds. "People apologize for things they're guilty of."

"Well, aren't I guilty?" I ask, still confused.

"Not anymore," He replies. "I've already forgiven you, James. That makes you guilt-free in my book. But I'll tell you what. If you really feel sorry about what happened, you'll have a lot of time this summer to clear your conscience. Building a barn isn't an easy task. Trust me."

I look at Mr. Peterson in bewilderment, hardly understanding his words as they leave his mouth.

Mr. Peterson looks at me for a moment and smiles, probably because of the dumbfounded look on my face. After a few seconds of silence, he shoots out his arm in my direction for a handshake. I shake his hand and return his smile with one of my own.

He turns back around to the bed of his pickup truck. I look at Mr. Peterson, then in the direction of where the barn once sat.

"So, where do we start?" I ask.

"With this," he replies, handing me what looks like a mix between a shovel and a bolt cutter.

CHAPTER SEVEN

"A shovel?" I ask, gripping the long wooden handles of the mysterious tool. "What are we digging?"

"Not a shovel, James. A post hole digger. Follow me and I'll show you," he says.

Mr. Peterson grabs a digger of his own from the bed of the old pickup and leads me in the direction of where the barn once stood.

"Do you remember how big my old barn used to be, James?" He asks, his arms confidently folded across his chest.

"Kind of," I reply. "I've only been here a few times — to buy firewood."

This isn't true, but I decide it's probably best not to tell Mr. Peterson about all the times the twins and I used to come here to play ball when we were younger.

"Well, the old barn was around twelve-hundred square feet and about thirty-five feet tall. Now, a big barn like that is heavy. Think about all the weight from the lumber, the hardware, the roofing. Well, a barn that big doesn't just stand up on its own. When I first built the barn, nearly fifty years ago, an old friend of mine, who happened to have much more building experience than I did, showed me how to start a project like this."

Mr. Peterson gets down on one knee and picks up a handful of what looks like freshly placed dirt. It's a different color than the rest of the dirt on the Peterson property — more orange than brown.

"I've had a busy last couple days here on the farm, James," Mr. Peterson begins, his eyes scanning the orange dirt in front of him. "The day after the accident, I had Earl Conway and his team come out here and help me get rid of all the burned pieces of wood, ash, and rubble, so that we could have a clean slate to work from. They helped me dump a couple truckloads of fresh dirt and spread it all out."

"So, what are the post hole diggers for?" I ask, still holding the heavy tool in my right hand.

"For those," Mr. Peterson answers, pointing in the direction of the stacked lumber. To the right of the two-by-fours lay about a dozen large, wooden beams. "Those are our posts, James. The plan for today is for you and me to measure out and plant fourteen posts in the ground.

We'll need to space out our posts evenly, dig holes for each one, raise the posts into the holes, and fill the holes with concrete so that our posts are nice and sturdy. How does that sound?"

"Sounds good to me," I answer.

We started our day of work doing nearly everything together. At first, I thought it was because Mr. Peterson didn't trust me to work on my own (I wouldn't blame him), but I later realized that each task was far too much work for either one of us to take on alone. We spent the first part of the day measuring out where we needed to dig post holes for the large wooden beams. After that, we carried the beams to their respective locations, Mr. Peterson on one end of a beam and me on the other. At one point, I complained about getting a splinter in my hand and Mr. Peterson responded by letting out a little laugh under his breath and then taking off his working gloves and handing them to me. At first, I was a little embarrassed to take the gloves from him, but after remembering how rough and tough his hands were compared to mine, I thanked him and slid the gloves over my own hands.

After each post was in its rightful place, the digging began. Mr. Peterson dug the first two holes himself with me watching before he released me to dig my own. It looked easy enough — until it was actually my turn. I was surprised by how easy he made it look. Mr. Peterson's post hole digger seemed to cut through the earth like butter, and mine seemed to cut through the earth like... well, earth.

After a few hours of digging and sweating, we finally had dug all fourteen post holes.

"You look terrible," Mr. Peterson says with a smile, walking in my direction.

"I *feel* terrible." I reply, matching his smile with one of my own. "You don't look so hot yourself."

Mr. Peterson laughs and inspects my most recent and final post hole.

"Looks really good, James," he says.

"Thanks. This is exhausting. I can't believe you built your last barn all by yourself," I say, wiping the beads of sweat from my forehead.

"Who ever said I built it by myself?" He asks, smiling in my direction.

"Oh, I don't know," I reply sheepishly. "I guess I just assumed that you did."

"No, no," he replies, looking off in the distance, a subtle smile sprawling across his lips. "I had help."

We were both quiet for a moment until Mr. Peterson broke the silence with a loud sigh and a stretch.

"Well, James. What are your lunch plans?" Mr. Peterson asks. "If you didn't bring anything, I'd love to have you over to the house."

"I was just planning on heading home and making a sandwich," I reply.

"Nonsense!" Mr. Peterson says, a smile still spread thickly on his face. "Hop in the truck and we'll head over to my place."

I make my way over to the passenger side of the pickup truck to get in. Before joining me in the cab of the truck, Mr. Peterson rummages through something in the bed of the pickup. After twenty seconds or so, he opens the driver side door with a couple of ice-cold bottles of water in his hands.

"You earned it," he says, handing me one of the bottles.

The drive to Mr. Peterson's home isn't very far. I can see his house in the distance. After driving down the old, dirt road for about a minute, we finally pull into the driveway. While I've been to the Peterson property on several occasions, either playing ball with the twins or buying firewood from the barn, I've never actually been outside Mr. Peterson's *home*, let alone inside of it.

Mr. Peterson's home is well taken care of, at least from the outside. A beautiful yard full of green grass surrounds the building, with the exception of the gravel driveway which cuts right through it. A white porch wraps around the entirety of the house. The pillars of the porch are ornate and look handcrafted. While there are a few spots on the old house that look as though they could use a touch of paint, the house is, for the most part, in excellent condition. The window shutters on both sides of the front door are painted with a deep, dark red which matches the color of the front door.

Mr. Peterson parks the truck in the gravel driveway and leads me up to the front door of the house.

"Now, don't mind the mess, young man," Mr. Peterson

says as we walk up the beautiful, white, wooden stairs of the porch. "I don't have visitors all too often."

Mr. Peterson turns the key in the lock and pushes the large, red door open.

CHAPTER EIGHT

As I walk through the doorway of Mr. Peterson's home, I don't see the messy interior that I had expected, but rather a well-kept, beautiful home that looks as though it had been decorated by an interior designer and cleaned regularly.

To the immediate right of the doorway is a line of beautiful wicker baskets filled with what look like hand-sewn quilts and several decorative pillows. Two brown leather couches form a ninety-degree angle in the living room and are draped with lovely, white throws. Most of the walls in Mr. Peterson's home are white, or perhaps off-white, with the exception of the wall leading into the dining room, which is slate blue.

"Wow, your house is —" I begin to say before Mr.

Peterson cuts me off.

"I know, I know," he interjects. "A little messy, huh?"

"No, no! I was just going to say that it's really nice. Did you decorate it yourself?"

"Oh, heavens no," he responds with a slight chuckle. "I'd have no idea where to even begin with decorating a home. No, this was all done by my lovely wife."

"I didn't know you were married," I admit as Mr. Peterson leads me to the dining room table and signals for me to take a seat.

"Well, I haven't been for a while. I lost Allison eight years ago, but I just haven't had the heart to change much around the house. Plus, I don't really mind all the ruffles and doilies as much as you might think. That's her in the photo there."

Mr. Peterson nods behind my shoulder in the direction of the china cabinet. Beneath a display of beautiful Blue Willow china is an arrangement of photo frames, Mrs. Peterson being in nearly every one of them.

"I'm sorry for your loss," I say.

"No, that's ok, son. Everyone goes sometime. That's the way life works. Plus, she was sick and getting up in years. She's happier up there with Jesus than she would be down here."

I'm a little surprised to hear Mr. Peterson say something so blatantly Christian, though I choose not to think too much of it. Something tells me it's not the right time to tell him that I don't believe in all that stuff.

Mr. Peterson makes a couple of ham and cheese sandwiches in the kitchen while I sit at the dining room table, still admiring his home and the many paintings and photos hung on the walls. Over lunch, he tells me more about his wife. He explains that they had met when they were only seventeen years old and began dating directly after graduating from high school.

Mr. Peterson takes a last bite of his sandwich, followed by a gulp of water from the mason jar in front of him. I so badly want to ask him about my grandpa. I begin to wonder if he even knows that I'm John Connor's grandson. I sit back in my chair and cross my arms.

"Mr. Peterson, Uncle Ira mentioned that you and my grandpa were friends," I say, my eyes locked on his.

He sets the jar down on the table in front of him and matches my stare with one of his own, followed by a smile across his old lips.

"More like brothers," Mr. Peterson says, sitting up straight in his chair.

"Really?" I ask, leaning in closer, listening more carefully now than I had all day.

Mr. Peterson looks at me in silence for a moment.

"Follow me, James. I want to show you something."

I stand up and follow Mr. Peterson out of the dining room and into the small, but well-decorated, living room next door. Mr. Peterson signals for me to take a seat on the leather sofa and walks over to the small bookshelf on the other side of the room. After rummaging through the bookshelf for a few minutes, he seems to finally find what he was looking for and comes to sit beside me.

In his hands is an old, leather scrapbook. He opens it, flipping through several pages until he gets near the end of the book. I notice that most of the photos are of Mr. and Mrs. Peterson, along with several faces that I don't recognize.

"Ah, here we are," he says, opening the book wide and setting it across my lap. "This is your grandpa John and me, here," he says pointing an old finger at one of the photos in the book.

I can hardly believe my eyes. I look just like my grandpa. He's a bit older than me in the photo, maybe in his late twenties or early thirties, but I can still see the obvious resemblance. In the photo, Mr. Peterson and my grandpa are both wearing plain white t-shirts, holding an entire stringer full of fish in front of a pond. It must be the pond on the Peterson property that Uncle Ira told me about.

"Wow, look at all those fish," I say, still amazed by the photo.

"Yeah, John was my favorite fishing buddy. He's one of the few men I'd never get tired of fishing with. He knew how to keep a conversation going while on the lake. Talking helps to catch more fish. It lets the fish know you're friendly."

I look over to Mr. Peterson to see him smile and chuckle at his own joke.

Mr. Peterson turns the page of the scrapbook and to my surprise, I see another photo of him with my grandpa. In this photo, the two of them are dressed up nicely, neckties and everything, and standing in front of a large, white building.

"Where was *this* photo taken?" I ask, trying to make out which building they were in front of.

"That's at North Pike Baptist Church, just outside of town. It was the day of your grandpa's baptism."

"Baptism?" I ask. "I didn't know Grandpa was a —"

"A Christian?" Mr. Peterson interjects, finishing my question for me. "Oh yes. In fact, the only thing your grandpa liked more than fishing was praying."

I look up at Mr. Peterson again, hardly believing my ears, then back down to the photo in the scrapbook. Why hadn't my parents or Uncle Ira or Aunt Terry ever told me that Grandpa was a Christian?

After hearing Mr. Peterson share a story or two more about "the old days" with my grandpa, it's finally time to get back to work. We head back to the construction site and work for several more hours. With every plank of wood we carry and every post hole we fill with concrete, the only thing on my mind is Grandpa.

CHAPTER NINE

It's been a month since the construction of the new barn began, though it feels as though it's only been a few days. For the past four weeks, I've met Mr. Peterson at the barn's construction site at eight o'clock every morning. However, this morning I'm supposed to meet him at his house, though I'm not entirely sure why.

I hop out of bed and follow my usual morning routine, before jogging down the stairs to say goodbye to Uncle Ira and Aunt Terry. When I finally make my way down, they're still seated at the table and seem to be finishing their breakfast.

"James, come eat something before you go!" Aunt Terry shouts in my direction before I have a chance to bolt out the door.

"Not this morning. Thank you for cooking and everything, but I'm already running late," I explain, eager to find out what's on the agenda for today.

"Well, here," Aunt Terry says, quickly hopping up from her seat and making her way to the kitchen counter. "At least take some breakfast to-go."

She grabs a paper bag from one of the drawers in the kitchen, lines it with paper towels and fills it with biscuits and sausage links.

"Have fun today, kiddo," I hear Uncle Ira say as Aunt Terry hands me the paper bag.

"I will. I'll be home around the usual time today," I say darting toward the front door.

I walk outside and head toward the Camry.

It's been a great few weeks and the barn is finally starting to take shape. Once we anchored all the posts in the post holes, we were able to start hammering two-by-four support beams from one post to another. Rather than looking like a bunch of random poles sticking up in the middle of a field, it's finally starting to look like a building. From what Mr. Peterson says, we'll likely be finished with the entire barn before the summer is over.

It isn't long before I drive onto the familiar gravel road of the Peterson property. However, this time, instead of turning right at the gate by the barn, I continue driving for about a minute until I pull onto Mr. Peterson's driveway. I walk up to the front door and knock, my brain spinning as to why he could possibly have wanted me to meet him here instead of at the barn.

I hear rustling in the house and the sound of footsteps growing louder in the direction of the front door. My curiosity is instantly dismissed as Mr. Peterson opens the door, a fishing pole in one hand and a full tackle box in the other. On Mr. Peterson's head is a fishing hat that looks to be as old as he is, several colorful lures hooked onto either side.

"Ready to take on the lake?" He asks, a huge smile spread wide across his face.

I don't know what to say. I don't have much fishing experience, though I have enjoyed it the few times I've gone with the twins. Anyway, I'd rather spend the morning fishing than lifting lumber and swinging a hammer.

"I'd love to!" I respond, taking the fishing pole from Mr. Peterson.

"That a boy!" he says. "Let me finish getting my gear together and we'll head down to the pond."

Mr. Peterson spends a couple more minutes inside, rummaging through a drawer. He comes back with another fishing rod for himself, as well as a pair of pliers and an old, wooden pocketknife. We hop in his pickup truck and make our way around to the back side of the house and onto a dirt road I've never seen before. After a few minutes on the gravel road, we finally emerge through the woods. Between the trees ahead, I can just make out a beautiful body of water.

"Does all of this belong to you?" I ask, admiring the

pond ahead of us.

"Oh no," he responds, looking at me and then back to the pond. "As far as I'm concerned, this pond belongs to God. But that," he says, gesturing toward a boat tied to a dock on the far, right edge of the pond. "*That* belongs to me."

The boat is small and old, though not so old that it looks unreliable. The once-blue paint is faded and a stripe of rust lines its top rim. As we get out of the truck and begin walking toward the boat, I can just barely make out a word in old, faded calligraphy, hovering just above the water line. "*Serenity.*"

Mr. Peterson leads us onto the dock and instructs me to carefully climb aboard while holding onto the dock railing with one hand.

"Is the name of the boat *Serenity*?" I ask, nodding in the direction of the faded paint.

"Indeed it is," he responds.

"That's an interesting name for a boat," I admit.

"It is? Why's that?" Mr. Peterson asks with a grin.

"I don't know," I say, matching his smile with my own. "Aren't boats usually named after women?"

"Some of them are," he responds, still smiling. "But I decided to name this particular boat after what I experience while in it — *Serenity.*"

I climb into the boat as Mr. Peterson loads in all of our fishing gear. He joins me and hands me a long, wooden paddle matching the one in his own hands.

It isn't long after paddling away from the old, wooden dock that I start to understand why Mr. Peterson named the boat what he did. I listen to the sound of birds chirping and feel the light breeze of the morning on my face. Coolness rises up from the water, but not so much that it feels *cold*. I look around at the trees surrounding the lake, realizing they're the same trees that my grandpa must have seen all those years ago.

"Have you been fishing before?" Mr. Peterson asks me as he begins baiting the hook at the end of my fishing rod with what looks like a lime-green, plastic worm.

"Not a lot," I admit. "Just once or twice with the twins when we were kids."

Mr. Peterson immediately stops fiddling with the hook in his hands and looks up at me.

"The Clements boys, huh?" he asks, still looking straight at me.

"Yes sir," I respond, this time more nervous. The way Mr. Peterson responds to my talking about the twins makes me feel as though he knows something about their involvement with the fire a few weeks ago.

"You're close with those boys, aren't you?" Mr. Peterson asks.

"Yes," I start. "Well, I mean, I used to be."

"Well, what happened, James?" he inquires further.

"Let's just say they weren't there for me when I needed them to be," I reply sheepishly.

Mr. Peterson finishes tying the hook onto the fishing

line and sets it carefully beside him on the seat of the boat.

"This wouldn't have anything to do with the fire at the barn a few weeks ago, would it?" he asks.

I don't know what to say. I made the decision not to rat out the twins and I intend to stick to my guns. But then again, what's the worst that could happen if I *did t*ell Mr. Peterson the truth? Could the twins even get in trouble at this point? After all, I'm already serving out the sentence and helping Mr. Peterson rebuild the barn.

I finally muster the courage to push a response through my mouth.

"I'd rather not say."

With a slow smile, Mr. Peterson nods his head and picks the hook and fishing line back up.

"I understand," he says. "It's hard when the people we care about do things that hurt us. So, do you think you'll ever get around to forgiving them?"

"I don't know," I say. "I mean, they were always my closest friends growing up. We go all the way back to the second grade. But it just seems like most of our friendship has been one-sided — the twins getting themselves into trouble, and me trying to get them out of it."

"Well, it sounds like you've been a good friend to *them*, at least," says Mr. Peterson.

We finally finish rigging our fishing lines and start doing what Mr. Peterson calls "lazy man fishing." We cast our lines out into the water as far as we can, lean our rods against the siding of the boat, and begin paddling. I'm skeptical at first. After all, anytime that I've seen anyone fish on TV, they always seem to cast and reel, over and over again. We don't paddle the boat forward for more than a minute before my skepticism vanishes. I hear a loud thud, and immediately look down to see the end of my fishing rod bend.

"Looks like you've got one!" Mr. Peterson shouts, smiling larger than normal.

Mr. Peterson instructs me on how to properly "set the hook" and I start reeling it in. I finally reel the fish all the way in — a little too far, in fact. Apparently, you aren't supposed to reel the fish in all the way to the tip of your rod.

"Smallmouth bass," Mr. Peterson says, identifying the fish as he starts working on removing the hook from its lip.

As he uses his silver pliers to remove the hook, I notice something about Mr. Peterson that I've never seen before — a scar, a long one, across the back of his right hand, extending from his thumb joint to his pinky.

Mr. Peterson releases the fish into the water. He must have seen me staring at his hand.

"Go ahead, son," he says, nodding his head toward me and then looking down at the scar on his hand. "You want to ask me how I got it?"

"I'm sorry," I say. "I didn't mean to —"

"No, no. That's ok," he responds, cutting me off. "It's been a long time since I've even thought about it. And anyways, you of all people deserve to hear the story."

"Really? Why *me?*" I ask.

"Well, because this was a gift from your grandfather."

"What?!" I ask, my voice a little higher pitched than normal. "My grandpa cut your hand open!?"

Mr. Peterson chuckles.

"Yes, though not intentionally," he explains. "You see, your grandfather and I used to do everything together. We'd fish together, go to church together, and build together. It really isn't much of a story. You see, one day your grandfather was helping me build a new door for my barn. We had bought all the lumber and hardware we needed and spent the entire afternoon cutting everything down to size. Well, we were about ten minutes from finishing the project when a rainstorm came out of nowhere. Two fellas smarter than us would have just waited for the rain to subside before finishing the project, but not your grandpa and me. You see, we had a lot in common, including our stubbornness.

With rain falling heavily around us, we finally hoisted up the new barn door and attached the new hardware to the building. After trying to shut the door, we realized we had cut it just a hair too wide, enough so that it wouldn't properly shut. Your grandfather, always willing to fix any problem, told me to press firmly against the door while he shaved some of the wood off of the side of the door with his pocketknife. He spent the next minute or so cutting away at the door, both of us getting drenched by the downpour. After one of his long jabs at the door, he accidentally started his cut a few inches too high, and sliced the back of my hand."

My eyes are wider than they've been all day. Noticing how silly I probably look with my jaw dropped the way it is, I try composing myself before asking my next series of questions.

"Did you have to go to the hospital? How long did it take to heal? Were you and Grandpa still friends after that?"

Mr. Peterson laughs.

"Of course we were still friends, James," Mr. Peterson answers with a smile. "When you're friends with someone — when you're *really* friends, you choose to forgive. The choice isn't always easy, but it's always necessary."

My mind races back to Scott and Sam. Should I forgive them for what they did? For letting me take the fall for something that was more their fault than mine? And for going on our trip without me? I don't think about it for more than twenty seconds before I know the answer. I need to make things right — not because it'll be easy, but because it's necessary.

The rest of the day flew by. Mr. Peterson and I stayed on the boat for nearly three hours, reeling in dozens of fish, mostly smallmouth bass. Soon after, we hopped back into Mr. Peterson's truck and came back to the house for a couple of sandwiches, before starting the day's work. Much like the past week or so, we spent the remaining hours of the day screwing two-by-fours across the support beams of the barn until the sun began to set.

"Thanks for taking me fishing today," I say to Mr.

Peterson, both of us walking away from the worksite, toward our vehicles.

"The pleasure was all mine, James," Mr. Peterson says, loading some of his tools into the bed of the pickup. "After all, fishing's always more fun with company!"

I start toward the Camry. I'm nearly sitting down when I feel something in my pocket — Mr. Peterson's pocketknife. I must have put it in my pocket during the fishing trip.

"Mr. Peterson! Your knife!" I shout, waving his knife in the air from the driver's side window of the Camry.

Mr. Peterson looks at me and then at the knife.

"Why don't you hold onto it, James?" He asks.

"Are you sure? It's *your* knife." I say, amazed that he would give his personal pocketknife to someone he had known for such a short period of time.

"Very sure," He replies. "I hardly ever use it at my age, and something tells me you'll get more years of use out of it than I will at this point!"

I thank Mr. Peterson and start down the gravel road in the direction of home. I can't wait to shower and get some rest. But not before I make things right with the twins.

CHAPTER TEN

I haven't been to Sam and Scott's house in weeks. It's already seven o'clock when I pull onto the cracked pavement of their driveway. I see the twins' Ford Explorer sitting under the overhang of the carport, to the right of Mr. and Mrs. Clements' brand new BMW. The sun is already beginning to set and as I crack open the driver's side door of the Camry, I can hear a symphony of crickets chirping from the woods in the twins' overgrown backyard.

The Clements' backyard brings back so many memories for me. Growing up, I'd often ride my bike here just as the twins were finishing their homework. The Clements only live ten or so minutes from Uncle Ira and Aunt Terry, which made being friends with Sam and Scott very convenient. Most days, I'd be welcomed inside and offered an ice-cold glass of Kool-Aid or a peanut butter sandwich. Mrs. Clements always made the best peanut butter sandwiches. She would toast the bread and spread butter on the insides of each slice before spreading the peanut butter on top. After eating a snack or two, the twins and I would all dart out the backdoor, down the wooden staircase of their back porch, to the trampoline, where we'd jump and play and laugh for hours. Our biggest worries were so small when we were that age — before the realities of life set in.

As I open the door of the Camry to get out, my heartbeat quickens. I haven't seen the twins since before the fire. I haven't even *spoken* to them. I walk up the stone walkway to the front porch and slowly and hesitantly make my way to the front door. I begin preparing myself for what they might say — and for what I might say. No matter what, I know that I need to forgive them.

I knock only three times before being answered by a voice.

"Just a moment!"

I can tell that the voice belongs to Mrs. Clements.

I hear footsteps approach the front door, followed by the sound of the lock being turned.

"James! What a great surprise. How are you?" Mrs. Clements asks.

"I'm ok," I reply with a smile.

I've always liked Mrs. Clements. It's *Mr. Clements* who can be a little more on the intimidating side. I've never really had to worry too much about that, though, since he's hardly ever home.

"I heard about everything with the barn," Mrs. Clements says.

"You did?" I ask.

"Yes and thank heavens that you're ok! It sounds like you could have been hurt. But I think it's so nice that you're doing the right thing to help that poor man rebuild it this summer!"

Mrs. Clements' response clearly indicates that Sam and Scott never admitted the truth, even to their own parents.

"Are the guys home?" I ask, now looking at my feet instead of at Mrs. Clements.

"They sure are. One minute, James."

"Boys! You've got company!" Mrs. Clements shouts down the hall. "They should be out in a minute. Come on inside!"

I walk slowly through the front door and enter into the large living room in front of me. To my right is a large wooden entertainment center with the Clements' huge, eighty-inch, flat screen television displayed proudly on top of it. The couch in the living room is a dark brown leather one with scuff marks all over it. It's the same couch they've had all these years. In fact, when we were all younger, I'd come over to spend the night from time to time and all three of us would sleep in this very living room together, after making a fort with the couch, a sheet, and a couple of chairs.

"Coming!" Sam shouts back, followed by the sounds

of feet jogging down the hallway.

"Who is —" Sam starts to ask, before being cut off by his own surprise.

"Oh, James," he says sheepishly. "How are you?"

I don't answer. Not yet.

Mrs. Clements must be able to tell that something isn't quite right, because after only a few seconds of silence, she makes an excuse about something burning in the kitchen and leaves us alone in the living room.

As Sam and I stand there quietly, looking at one another, I hear a door slam down the hallway, followed by another set of footsteps.

"Well, look who it is," Scott says sarcastically, making his way into the living room.

I take a deep breath.

"Hey fellas," I say. "Can we talk for a minute?"

Scott and Sam both look at each other and then look back to me.

"Sure," Sam answers.

I look in the direction of the kitchen for a moment.

"Maybe we could talk out on the porch?" I ask.

The three of us walk past Mrs. Clements in the kitchen and in the direction of the back door which leads to the twins' large, screened-in back porch. The outside air is cooler than it was only minutes ago, and the sun has already fallen beneath the horizon, exposing the stars in the sky above us.

I look in the direction of the Clements' old grill on

the far side of the porch. They've had the grill for as long as I can remember. The words "Broil King" stretch across the front of the grill's metal hood and rust lines the entirety of its siding. Directly in front of the grill is a large burn mark on the wooden porch, with a width of about two feet. It happened when the three of us were only twelve years old. I had watched a tv show where a magician had used lighter fluid to make a huge fire on the ground, without burning anything. He was even able to light his hand on fire without feeling any pain. One day, at the twins' house, I had the idea to try it. We grabbed some of Mr. Clements' lighter fluid and squirted nearly two cups of it into a puddle on the Clements' back porch. Needless to say, we couldn't put the fire out in time, and what ended up being left at the end of our stunt was none other than a two-feet-wide burn mark in the middle of the porch. Mr. Clements came home later that night and, after inspecting the burn mark, was furious. I'll never forget what Scott and Sam did. They immediately took all the blame for the fire and for the burn mark and told their dad that they had done it hours before I had even arrived that evening.

"What brings *you* here?" Sam asks, a serious look plastered across his face.

"Yeah, are you here to rat us out to our folks?" Scott blurts out, a nasty look on his face.

Sam gives his brother a look of disapproval that I've seen too many times before.

"No," I answer, arms folded, looking Scott square in

the eye.

"You're not?" Scott asks, this time with a less nasty tone in his voice.

"Nope. I'm not here to tell your parents about the barn, or the fire, or anything else," I explain.

The twins look surprised.

"Well, James," Sam starts. "What exactly *are* you here for?"

I take a deep breath before answering.

"I'm here to tell you both that I'm sorry."

The twins' faces have never looked more surprised.

"What in the world are *you* sorry about? James, we're the ones who ditched you and let you take the fall for the fire all on your own," Sam says.

"I'm sorry for not being more responsible in the first place," I start. "I shouldn't have agreed to it. And I'm sorry for choosing the Peterson property. I thought it would be safer than lighting them off in the woods, but I — I didn't know that —"

"None of us could have known," Sam says, cutting me off.

"James," Scott starts. "I — I really should be the one apologizing. The whole thing was my idea and I've been a pretty lousy friend to you these past few weeks."

I uncross my arms and stick my hands into my pockets.

"Apology accepted," I say, smiling, walking in the direction of the twins with my hand extended for a handshake.

The twins look at each other, smile, then look back at me. They both dart forward to be the first one to shake my hand.

"I guess you could say this has been my way of paying you back for the last fire," I say, smiling.

The twins look confused, so I glance down and nod in the direction of the burn mark in front of the grill.

The twins and I laughed and caught up for the next hour and a half. I explained to them all that I had learned by helping Mr. Peterson rebuild the barn and they told me about their trip to Florida.

"It would have been way more fun if you had been there," they kept saying.

After catching up for a while, I told the twins I needed to head home to get some rest. I drove home, trudged my way up the long, wooden staircase, and climbed immediately into my bed. For the first time in several weeks, I closed my eyes and fell asleep instantly.

CHAPTER ELEVEN

It's been a couple of days since my visit to Scott and Sam's house. It's funny. Just a handful of days ago, I felt as though it wouldn't bother me much to never see the two of them again (they probably felt the same way), but now things seem back to normal, almost as if nothing had ever happened.

The barn is starting to look great. We haven't gotten around to painting it yet, so it looks more like a large shed than a barn. But, once we paint the building with the deep red paint in the back of Mr. Peterson's truck, I'm sure it'll start to look just like his old barn.

Today, Mr. Peterson and I are hanging the barn's front doors. He told me this morning that he wanted to use a sliding barn door this time, rather than a traditional door like he had on his last barn. We're already about halfway finished hanging the door's hardware.

"Once we get this hardware secured against this front wall, hanging the door will be a breeze," explains Mr. Peterson from the top of his ladder, extending his hand toward me for another screw.

I reach down into the large, white bucket of miscellaneous nails and screws, looking for another long one to hand to Mr. Peterson. Today is hot — one of the hottest days we've had in months. This morning, Uncle Ira mentioned that he heard the weatherman say something about the drought getting worse before it gets better. I can't remember the last time it rained.

"What do you think about all this heat?" I ask Mr. Peterson from the bottom of the ladder, looking up at him with squinted eyes to avoid staring directly into the sun.

"It's been plenty hot lately, that's for sure," he answers.

I've never been great at small talk. Everyone always thinks that I'm shy or introverted, and maybe I am a little. But I'm mostly just quiet because I don't have much to say most of the time.

"Do you want me to grab your bottle of water for you?" I ask, starting in the direction of the work bench toward my own water bottle.

"I'll do you one better," Mr. Peterson replies, climbing slowly down the ladder, sweat dripping from his face.

"How about a lemonade break?"

Mr. Peterson and I climb into his pickup and start

toward his house at the end of the long gravel road. Within a few minutes we're in Mr. Peterson's kitchen — well, he's in the kitchen. I'm sitting down, exhausted at the dining room table.

"How are you not totally exhausted?" I ask. "You were the one on the ladder hanging the hardware. I was only handing you screws and tools when you asked for them, and I'm so tired I feel like I can hardly move."

"Well, James," Mr. Peterson starts. "After you've built as many barns and sheds and chairs and tables as I have, things start to become second nature for you. I guess you could say I'm more comfortable *with* a hammer than I am *without* one at this point!"

Mr. Peterson smiles in my direction as he opens the fridge and pulls out a half full pitcher of lemonade.

"You build tables and chairs?" I ask. "I thought Peterson Lumber only sold firewood."

"Well, it does. Though, that wasn't the plan from the start. You see, when I was younger, I had this dream of opening a small country store, selling chairs and tables and dressers — really anything made from wood. Over the years, I guess I've just gotten so busy that I never really felt like the time was right to change the way I do business."

"I never knew that about you," I say. "I'd love to see some of your work."

"You're sitting in it!" Mr. Peterson replies with a chuckle.

I look down at the chair I'm sitting in, realizing for

the first time that it's handcrafted. In fact, all the chairs around Mr. Peterson's dining room table are handcrafted, matching the same wood and finish as the large table to the right of me.

"You made these chairs? And this table?" I ask, amazed.

"Look around the house, son," Mr. Peterson answers, pouring lemonade into the two glass mason jars on the counter. "Anything you see around here that's made of wood was built with these two, old hands."

I take my eyes off the dining room table and scan the rest of Mr. Peterson's home. A coffee table, two end tables, a mantle over Mr. Peterson's fireplace, a spice rack in the kitchen, a shoe rack to the left of the front door and several other items around the house. All wood. All handmade. All made by Mr. Peterson.

"Well, it's not too late to start building and selling furniture now, is it? If it was your dream, why don't you just do it?"

"Oh, James," Mr. Peterson starts. "It's not as simple as that. I'm getting old, my eyes aren't as good as they once were, and I'm afraid that —"

Mr. Peterson stops talking as he sits down next to me at the dining room table, pushing one of the mason jars full of lemonade toward me.

"Well, I guess I'm just afraid," he admits, looking away from me and out the dining room window. "And that's all I'd like to say about that."

I apologize and change the subject.

"I visited the twins a couple days ago," I say, taking a sip of the lemonade in front of me.

"The Clements boys, huh?" Mr. Peterson asks. "How did that go?"

"Good," I answer.

"What was the purpose of the visit?" Mr. Peterson asks, looking away from the window and back at me.

"Well, a while back, Sam and Scott and I had a falling out. But I remembered what you had said about you and Grandpa and how, even after he had cut your hand, you forgave him. I guess I figured life's too short not to forgive, especially when it's someone you care about."

Mr. Peterson takes a sip of lemonade from the jar in front of him and smiles a toothy smile in my direction.

"I couldn't have said it better myself, James."

Mr. Peterson and I sat in his kitchen for another twenty minutes or so, catching our breath and drinking lemonade. After that, we hopped back into the old pickup and headed back toward the barn to finish hanging the door. The rest of the process for hanging the barn door was pretty simple. Once we attached the hardware to the building and a few other pieces of hardware to the top of the door itself, we were able to slide the door into place with ease. After another ten minutes, the barn door was successfully hung, and slid open and closed perfectly.

"Well, I wish it would've been this easy to hang the doors on my last barn," Mr. Peterson says, taking a step back and admiring the tall, wooden building in front of us.

"I couldn't have done it without you."

"It seems like it would be near impossible for one person to handle a project like this alone," I say. "Is that why you had to have my grandpa's help with the last door?"

"Well, that was a different type of door we hung on the last barn," Mr. Peterson explains. "But yes, different type or not, hanging a door as large as this one requires at least one other set of hands."

"When we had first started rebuilding the barn, you mentioned that you didn't build the first barn on your own, but that you had help," I say, looking away from the barn and now at Mr. Peterson's tired face. "Who did you build your first barn with?"

Mr. Peterson is quiet for a moment. He takes the dirty, yellow work gloves off his hands and sticks them in his back pocket.

"It's funny you should ask me that, James," he starts. "When I had first moved to Thomasville all those decades ago, I didn't really know anyone. I was a young fellow, probably only ten years or so older than you are now. I had just bought all of this land out here and knew that I wanted to build myself a barn — a place to be the storefront for my country store."

Mr. Peterson takes a deep breath and looks again at the barn towering over us.

"It's a shame that the only wood that was ever sold here was the kind that people burn," Mr. Peterson starts. "In any case, I didn't know many people in Thomasville yet, and I knew I needed an extra set of hands. One day I was filling up the old pickup with gas — it was actually at Edmund's down the street, only back then it was called Zebo's Gas Stop. I had become acquaintances with Zebo, the owner, over time and was telling him that I was planning on building a barn but needed an extra hand. Little did I know that our conversation was being overheard by your grandpa."

"That's where you met Grandpa?" I ask quickly. "At Edmund's?"

"Oh yes," Mr. Peterson answers. "The two of us spent the next several months together, building the barn from scratch. You see, he was a few years older than me, and already had some experience in construction. He taught me everything I know about building a barn."

The two of us look at each other for a moment and then look back to the barn.

"It's really coming together," I say, my arms folded proudly across my chest.

"Yes, it is, James." Mr. Peterson answers, a smile spread thickly across his face.

"It'll be just as good a barn as the last one, won't it?" I ask.

"Better than the last one," Mr. Peterson says.

"Better? Why's that?" I ask.

"James, my last barn was getting old. You remember seeing all those broken windows and rotted boards, don't you? Sometimes it's not enough to simply repair something.

Sometimes you have to rebuild from the ground up."

As we finish our work for the day, I thank Mr. Peterson for the lemonade, and start toward the Camry. Before I make it halfway to the vehicle, I hear Mr. Peterson call out to me from the barn.

"James!" Mr. Peterson shouts, walking quickly toward me.

"Yes?" I ask, turning around and walking back toward him.

"What are you doing tomorrow?" he asks.

"Tomorrow? Tomorrow's Sunday."

"I know that," he answers. "Do you have any plans?"

The truth is, I *don't* have plans. On Sundays, I normally stay home, help Uncle Ira cook a big breakfast, and either watch TV or help Aunt Terry run errands for most of the day.

"I don't. Why do you ask?"

Mr. Peterson smiles and takes another step in my direction.

"Why don't you meet me at my place tomorrow morning? Around ten o'clock. I want to show you something."

I agree and shake Mr. Peterson's hand one last time before returning to the Camry.

CHAPTER TWELVE

It's nearly ten o'clock as I pull onto the Peterson property's long, winding, dirt road. I'm unsure of what Mr. Peterson has in store for today. I doubt we're going to work on the barn, especially after all the progress we made yesterday. Maybe Mr. Peterson wants to surprise me with another fishing trip at the old pond behind his house.

I drive another minute down the gravel road and pull into the driveway to Mr. Peterson's house. I walk up the steps of the porch and ring the doorbell to let Mr. Peterson know that I'm here. I listen for footsteps and don't hear anything, so I decide to knock instead. After my third knock, I hear Mr. Peterson walking toward the door.

I'm surprised at Mr. Peterson's outfit as he opens the door. I've never seen him dressed up before. Normally when we're working, he wears a plain white t-shirt with blue jeans. This morning Mr. Peterson is wearing a fancy, blue, button-down shirt tucked tightly into a pair of nice pants.

"Hey there, James," Mr. Peterson says, opening the red front door.

"Morning," I say in response.

I look down at the worn out, black Nike's around my feet.

"Something tells me I'm a little underdressed for whatever we're doing today."

"Nonsense! You look great," he assures me.

Mr. Peterson invites me inside and motions for me to take a seat on the living room sofa.

"I'm guessing we aren't fishing today?" I ask, watching Mr. Peterson pull an old, leather book off of the bookshelf by the fireplace.

"No, we're not," he responds with a smile.

Mr. Peterson comes over to the sofa and takes a seat beside me.

"Yesterday, as we started talking about your grandpa, it made me think — you probably would enjoy seeing the place that meant more to him than anywhere else."

I look at Mr. Peterson again, still a little confused. It isn't until I look down at the tattered, leather book in Mr. Peterson's hands that I realize where we're going today. The book has the tail end of a faded, red bookmark peeking out from its pages. While the leather cover of the book is old and cracked, I can still read the words toward the top of the leather cover — Holy Bible. Mr. Peterson is taking me to church.

I've never been to church before. When the twins and I were in fourth grade, there was a kid in our class, Ethan, who went to church. He talked about it all the time. He and his family would go to church not only on Sundays, but several days during the week. I can't imagine being so interested in any building that I'd want to show up there so many days per week if I didn't have to.

After climbing into Mr. Peterson's truck, it doesn't take more than eight or nine minutes before we pull into the parking lot of the church. We're greeted by an old white sign with faded, black letters that read "North Pike Baptist Church." The white paint on the sign is peeling so much that it shows just as much bare wood as it does white paint. There aren't as many cars in the parking lot as I was expecting. Normally, when I think of the word "church," I think of a huge building filled to the brim with people. This building is rather small and looks to be fairly old. We pull the truck into a parking spot on the side of the building. As the gravel crunches beneath the wheels of Mr. Peterson's truck, I begin feeling a little sick to my stomach. I don't really want to go into the church, but I suppose I owe it to Mr. Peterson after all that he's done for me. Plus, it will be neat to see the building that my grandpa loved so much. Who knows, I may even end up sitting in the exact spot where he sat all those years ago.

As we walk toward the large double doors of the church building, I begin noticing the other people walking toward the church. I look down once again at my worn-out shoes, feeling both underdressed and underprepared. A friendly young couple is waiting at the front doors of the building, greeting visitors as they enter.

"Good morning!" They both shout in unison, each of them sticking an arm out for Mr. Peterson and me to shake. We shake their hands and walk into the old building.

Upon entering the church, we're instantly greeted by a large, open room filled from front to back with long, wooden benches for people to sit in. At the very front of the room is a stage, like something you'd see at a concert, only much smaller. My eyes scan the stage and notice a couple of instruments, some microphones, and a short little table near the front of the stage with a few books (probably Bibles) stacked on top of it. Behind the instruments, at the very back of the stage, is a dark brown, wooden cross.

Although I've never been to a church myself, I've seen them in movies and on TV. This particular church looks a little different than the ones I've seen in the movies. It's older and not quite as nice.

"I'll give you a tour of the church after the service," Mr. Peterson says, putting an arm on my right shoulder. "But first, we'd better find ourselves a good place to sit!"

Mr. Peterson leads us into the large room, clearing a path around the dozens of people standing in the center aisle between two rows of long, wooden benches. We quietly slide our way into a few open spots on one of the benches when the musicians on stage begin playing.

"Good morning!" says one of the musicians on stage. This particular musician is playing acoustic guitar. He has a long black beard that has grown out to about halfway down his chest. He's wearing tight denim jeans and a black, collared, short-sleeve shirt with the ends of his sleeves rolled up slightly.

"Good morning!" the congregation echoes back.

"We're about to hear the word of the Lord," the guitarist starts. "But first, let's spend some time worshipping our Lord and Savior, Jesus Christ. If you don't mind, let's all stand together and worship."

The guitarist looks over at the rest of the musicians on stage and gives a subtle nod in their direction. They begin playing together and, to my surprise, it actually sounds pretty good. I'm not sure what kind of music I expected them to play, but it seems like in the movies, church music is always boring and quiet.

Though I don't know the words to the songs, I tap my hand on the wooden bench in front of me, keeping time and nodding my head to the rhythm. Not only do I not *know* the words, but I also don't really understand many of them either. A few times, during the music portion of the service, I catch Mr. Peterson glance in my direction and smile. I'm not sure if he's smiling because he can tell I'm confused or if he's smiling because he's happy I came with him today.

When the band finishes their final song, another man slowly walks onto the stage. He's dressed much nicer than the bearded guitarist. He's wearing a white button-down shirt tucked tightly into a pair of nice slacks. His shoes are brown and shiny, and his hair is combed neatly across the top of his head.

"Thanks, Brian. Thanks, worship team," the man says, making his way to the microphone stand at the front of the stage.

"Isn't God good?" the man asks the congregation, his arms lifted high above his head.

"Amen!" everyone shouts back.

"You can all be seated now," he says. "If we haven't met yet, my name is Pastor Chris. I'm the Lead Pastor here at North Pike Baptist Church."

Pastor Chris seems friendly. His voice is calm and relaxed, and he has a friendly face. It's hard to tell exactly how old he is, though he seems to be in his early to mid-thirties.

After sharing some announcements, Pastor Chris instructs everyone to open their Bibles to a particular section. I look around as everyone starts flipping quickly through the pages in their books and feel a little embarrassed that I didn't bring one of my own. I think Mr. Peterson can tell that I feel out of place. He opens his own Bible to the right spot and subtly places it in my lap.

Pastor Chris starts by reading aloud from his Bible and then begins teaching, every now and then glancing at the Bible to read another line of text. I try to listen as he teaches, but my mind wanders. I think about the fire. About the barn. About the twins. About Grandpa. I begin daydreaming, my gaze fixed lifelessly on the acoustic guitar planted on the right side of the stage. Every now and then, I catch myself drifting off to sleep. It isn't that I don't like what Pastor Chris is saying. In fact, everything sounds really nice. He teaches about love and caring for one another and giving to those who need it. I don't mind his teaching at all, but for some reason my eyes grow heavier and heavier.

My attention is quickly won back as I hear a loud "thud" come from the direction of the stage. Pastor Chris drops a large, wooden chair from the edge of the stage onto the floor below. He removes the microphone from the stand in front of him and hops off the stage, walking over to the chair.

"Earlier, we learned the reason that God sent His son, Jesus, to Earth in the first place, was because of His great love for us," Pastor Chris begins. "He loved us so much that He wanted us to be reconnected with Him and for our relationship with Him to be restored. We talked about how without Jesus's sacrifice, we're all destined to spend eternity in Hell, because we're sinful people in a sinful world. We talked about Jesus's life and ministry on this earth and how He died on the cross for you and me, taking our shame, so that we can become blameless in God's eyes and spend eternity in Heaven with Jesus, worshipping Him."

Pastor Chris walks behind the wooden chair in front

of the stage and plants his hands firmly on the chair's back. He pauses a moment, looks down at the chair and then back to the congregation.

"So," he starts. "You're probably wondering why I threw a chair off the stage."

The smile on his face is received with a handful of chuckles from the crowd.

"Jesus's gift of eternal life isn't something we can earn. In fact, you and I both know that there's nothing we can do to make God love us *more,* and there's nothing we can do to make Him love us any *less.* Salvation isn't something we can *win* but is instead a free gift from God."

My eyes are locked on Pastor Chris. I've heard people mutter about Jesus and the cross a few times, but I've never really spent time trying to really understand the story. I find myself listening intently, eagerly anticipating what he'll say next.

"However," Pastor Chris continues, walking from one side of the chair to the other. "That doesn't mean that we're automatically saved when we're born. There's still something very important that we need in order to have this eternal life with Jesus. John 3:16 tells us that 'whoever believes in Him shall not perish, but have eternal life.' In order for us to receive this free gift from God, you and I must first believe in Him and accept Him into our hearts."

Pastor Chris pauses again, looking down at the chair once more.

"Let me ask you this. When you're tired of standing

up and you want to take a seat, what do you do?"

Everyone is quiet for a moment, perhaps thinking that Pastor Chris's question is a rhetorical one. Eventually, a man in the back of the room pipes up.

"You sit down!" the man yells. The answer is met with a room full of chuckles.

"Are you sure you don't inspect the chair first?" Pastor Chris asks, getting down on his hands and knees, as if to be inspecting the chair. "Of course, you don't. You believe that the chair will hold you up. It's second nature. Well, that's what it means to believe in Jesus. You trust Him. You may not be able to see Him with your eyes or feel Him with your hands. But you *believe* in Him with your heart. And once you believe in Him and accept Him into your heart, he's there to stay."

It wasn't long before Pastor Chris finished the rest of his sermon, and the band came back onto stage to sing two more songs. After a final prayer, the congregation was dismissed, and everyone began making their way out of the building and back to their vehicles. After ten minutes or so, the building was mostly empty, and it was time for Mr. Peterson to give me the tour of the church.

"And this is the very spot where your grandpa and I always sat," Mr. Peterson explains, placing his hands on the backs of one of the benches on the very right side of the room. "I would always sit here at the very end of the pew and your grandpa would sit right next to me."

"Wow," I answer, admiring the bench.

"What about your wife?" I ask. "Did she sit here, too?"

Mr. Peterson is quiet for a moment. I watch as he looks long and hard at the bench in front of him.

"Sometimes," he replies.

I'm about to ask a follow up question when we get interrupted by a familiar voice. It's Pastor Chris.

"Good morning, Chip!" Pastor Chris says, walking over to both of us with a smile on his face.

Pastor Chris looks different up close. Now that he's only a few feet from us, I can tell that he's older than I had originally thought.

"Morning, Chris!" Mr. Peterson answers in an equally chipper tone. "Chris, I want you to meet an incredible young man. This is James Connor. He's the grandson of John Connor."

Pastor Chris's smile widens as he extends his arm for a handshake.

"Well, it's great to meet you, James," he says.

"It's great to meet you, too. I really liked your speech," I say, trying my best to match his enthusiasm.

Pastor Chris lets out a little laugh and thanks me for the compliment. He then goes on to ask me several questions. He asks me where I grew up, what I like to do for fun, and when I think I'll be back to visit the church again.

"I'm not sure," I respond.

My response to Pastor Chris's question is a genuine

one. I'm not sure. About anything. I'm not sure when I'll come back to visit the church. I'm not sure about everything that I heard him talk about today. I'm not sure why I should become a Christian or if I even want to. I'm not sure why my grandpa decided to become one. In fact, at this moment, I'm the most unsure I've been in a long time.

After talking with Pastor Chris for a few more minutes, Mr. Peterson finishes giving me the tour of the church, and the two of us hop back into the truck to head back to Mr. Peterson's house. I thank him for inviting me to church, climb inside the Camry, and begin heading back home.

CHAPTER THIRTEEN

It's nearly two o'clock in the afternoon when I finally pull back into our old, familiar driveway. It looks as though Uncle Ira and Aunt Terry are both home, probably cleaning up after cooking a big lunch. I pull the Camry into its designated spot, on the far-right side of the driveway.

As I exit the car and begin walking toward the front door of the house, my eyes gravitate toward the roof. The gutters above are full to the brim with pine straw and old, dead leaves. When I was in middle school, cleaning the gutters was always my chore, though it never really felt much like a chore. I actually enjoyed it. Once per month, usually on a Saturday, I would wake up extra early in the morning, pull Uncle Ira's extension ladder out from the shed on the side of the house, and climb eagerly onto the roof. I'd pull a pair of work gloves over my hands and begin digging out wet clumps of leaves and pine straw. It would only take me around half an hour to clean the gutters on the entire front and back of the house. When I would finish, I wouldn't come down right away. I liked being up there on the roof, looking out over our lawn, at the cars down below. I felt invincible.

I walk up the porch stairs and make my way inside the house.

"There you are, Sport!" Uncle Ira says with a smile as I walk through the door. "You missed a big lunch, today. What have you been up to?"

I look at Uncle Ira and Aunt Terry. They're sitting on the living room couch, facing the fire. We don't typically light the fireplace during the summer, but every now and then Uncle Ira will get in the mood for a fire. I watch as the flames flicker back and forth, pushing against one another while the embers of the wood glow bright red under the heat of the flames.

"I was with Mr. Peterson," I answer, making my way into the fire-lit room.

"On a Sunday?" Aunt Terry asks. "Wow, that man sure is making the most of this arrangement, isn't he?" She shoots a wink my way.

"Well, we weren't working on the barn today," I explain.

"Oh, another fishing trip, then?" asks Uncle Ira.

"No," I answer. "He wanted to take me to his

church today. It was actually pretty neat."

Uncle Ira slowly puts down the newspaper he was reading, folding it up neatly and setting it on the coffee table to the side of the couch. Aunt Terry fiddles with the coffee mug in her hand, twisting it slowly from side to side. Both sets of eyes are locked on me.

"Church?" asks Uncle Ira. "James, you've never been interested in church before."

I pause for a moment before responding.

"Well, I wouldn't say I'm interested *now*, either," I answer. "Mr. Peterson just wanted to show me the church that he and Grandpa used to attend."

Uncle Ira and Aunt Terry look at one another with solemn faces.

"What else did Mr. Peterson tell you about your grandfather, James?" Uncle Ira asks.

At first, I'm confused by his question, but then I realize what he's asking.

"You mean about him being a Christian?" I ask in response.

Uncle Ira picks up his own cup of coffee from the table and takes a long sip. Neither of them respond to my question.

"Mr. Peterson told me that Grandpa was a Christian and that they would sit together at church. He showed me the bench they would sit on and the baptismal pool where —"

I'm cut off by Aunt Terry's voice, now more

monotone than it had been before.

"James," she starts. "Why don't you and Mr. Peterson spend more time focusing on getting the barn fixed and less time talking about all this church stuff?"

"Your aunt has a point, James," Uncle Ira says. "Going to church with Chip on Sundays wasn't part of the deal. All you're required to do is help him get his barn back up and running."

I feel my teeth clench together and my muscles begin tensing up. I don't know why I feel the urge to defend Mr. Peterson, but I do. After all, he's been nothing but kind to me. It's not like they really even know anything about him. Plus, they have no right to tell me what I can and can't do. If I want to go to church *every* Sunday with Mr. Peterson, I will. It's my life.

"Why does it matter to you what I choose to do with my own time on Sunday?" I ask, my voice getting louder. "What if going to church with Mr. Peterson was *my* idea? What if *I* wanted to see where Grandpa spent so much of his time? I'm learning more about my own grandfather from Mr. Peterson than I ever have from the two of you."

I can tell my words have offended Uncle Ira and Aunt Terry. I can't even remember the last time I raised my voice to them. I take a deep breath and try to compose myself. My eyes shift off Uncle Ira and Aunt Terry and over to the fire once again.

"James," starts Uncle Ira. "I'm sorry that you feel that we haven't told you enough about your grandfather.

He was a good man. He loved his family. He loved us. He loved *you*. I know that you were only a couple of years old when he passed on, but he was so proud to be your grandpa."

I wipe my hand along my right eye, keeping a tear from rolling down the side of my face.

"Then why doesn't anyone ever talk about him?" I ask. "Why does everything about Grandpa have to always feel like some big secret?"

Aunt Terry sets her coffee mug down and clears her throat, appearing to choke back a few tears of her own.

"As Ira said, your grandpa was a good man," she starts. "But there were certain things that he believed that rubbed the rest of the family the wrong way. It sounds like you're aware of him being a Christian. Well, he believed that anyone who *wasn't* a Christian like him was going to end up going to hell and suffering in fire for eternity. He would talk about it at family dinners. He would talk about it at birthday parties. He was so stubborn about his faith, that it began driving the rest of us away. It wasn't long before we stopped inviting him to family dinners altogether. Don't get us wrong, James. We would still visit him from time to time, but we would keep our visits short and our conversations even shorter."

"James," Uncle Ira starts. "It wasn't just the fact that your grandfather went to church or believed in some supernatural being. It was the fact that church and Jesus were the *only* things he ever talked about. That's why we've tried our best to raise you the way that we have. We wanted to keep you away from all that stuff until you were old enough to make up your mind for yourself."

I don't know how to respond to Uncle Ira or Aunt Terry. They obviously think that Grandpa was wrong in his beliefs. But Grandpa obviously thought that everyone else in our family was wrong. Someone has to be right.

"Well, what if *you're* wrong?" I ask. "What if my mom and dad were wrong? What if our whole family was wrong and Grandpa was *right?* What if there actually *is* a God?"

I answer my own question internally as I feel the heat from the fireplace on my face.

"James, we've raised you better than to believe in this nonsense," Uncle Ira answers, his voice now growing louder and more impatient. "You can go to church all you want. You can read the Bible. You can pray. You and Mr. Peterson can sing Kumbaya all day long, but none of that is going to change the facts. The facts are that God doesn't exist and there isn't some scary place full of fire where bad people go and some happy place in the clouds where good people go."

My mind instantly shifts to what Pastor Chris talked about this morning. If Heaven *does* exist, it isn't a place where "good people" go. It's a place where people go when they believe in Jesus.

"How can you so easily discredit something that you don't even understand?" I ask, turning around and quickly stomping away from Uncle Ira and Aunt Terry.

"Where are you going, James?" Aunt Terry asks.

"To bed," I say, quickly.

"It's only three o'clock," she says.

I don't respond.

CHAPTER FOURTEEN

The heat of the summer sun presses against the back of my neck as I continue pushing the wet paint roller up and down, against the bare wood of the barn. I pause for a moment to admire my work. A couple of days ago, I never would have thought that I'd be able to paint like this. My work isn't perfect, but it's also not too bad. There are a couple of obvious drip marks and a few spots where I can see the layers of paint overlap. I walk around to the other side of the barn to see Mr. Peterson's progress. As I round the corner, I'm amazed at his work. No drips. No overlapping. I can also tell by his progress that he's much faster at painting than I am.

"I still can't believe how good you are at all this stuff," I say, still holding the paint roller in my right hand.

Mr. Peterson continues rolling for a moment, lifting his arms as high above his head as he can to reach a new spot of bare wood.

"Well, I wasn't always good at it, James," he responds, turning his head and smiling in my direction. "Practice makes perfect. Just a couple more barns and you'll be as good as me!" He chuckles at his own joke before coughing into his hands.

Mr. Peterson seems to be more short of breath than normal. He sets his paint roller down into the tray of dark red paint.

Today has been a productive day. The barn has been completely built now for a couple of days and we're over halfway done with the painting. The past few days have been so busy, my mind has been distracted from the fight I had with Uncle Ira and Aunt Terry. I know that I probably should apologize for the way I acted, but in some ways, it seems easier to just forget about it and move on.

"It looks like we're almost finished," I say, walking toward Mr. Peterson's pickup truck to grab an ice-cold water bottle from the cooler in the bed of the truck.

"You want one?" I ask, rummaging through the cold ice.

Mr. Peterson doesn't answer. He probably didn't hear me. I stop sifting through the ice and ask again. He still doesn't answer, so I decide to grab him one anyways. I pull two cold bottles of water from the cooler and turn around to start walking back. It isn't until I'm halfway back to the barn that I look up to see Mr. Peterson bending over, gripping his chest with his right hand.

I drop the water bottles onto the earth beneath me and run toward him.

"What's wrong!?" I ask, still sprinting in his direction.

Mr. Peterson doesn't answer, but turns toward me, his body trembling and his hands shaking violently. The look on his face is terrifying. I've never seen Mr. Peterson look so afraid. His eyes are bloodshot, and his lips are quivering. Still gripping his chest with his right hand, he slowly lifts his shaky left hand and points toward the pickup truck.

"Phone..." he manages to say, in an out-of-breath, hoarse voice. "Call 911."

Without waiting another moment, I sprint toward the pickup truck to get Mr. Peterson's phone to call 911. I would use my own phone, but my car is parked further away, closer to the wooden fence at the entrance of the field. My mind is racing. I've never seen someone have a heart attack in real life, though I've heard plenty of stories about people who have had them. Only a handful of seconds pass before I finally reach the pickup. I begin rummaging through the truck to find Mr. Peterson's cell phone. I can't find it right away. I look on the dash and in the middle console between the two seats. I start to grow panicked. Finally, I feel a rush of relief as I flip down the driver's side visor and watch as Mr. Peterson's phone falls quickly onto the seat below it.

I pick up the phone and dial 911 as quickly as I can.

CHAPTER FIFTEEN

The waiting room of the hospital is less crowded than I thought it would be. I look across the brightly lit room and see a young couple sitting together in the corner. They have two children with them, a boy and a girl, who seem to be making a large tower out of Legos.

The walls of the waiting room are painted a light cream color, and the lights in the room are mainly fluorescent, with the exception of a small lamp with a warm glow sitting on a coffee table in the corner. The waiting room chairs are all the same shade of green and are arranged in small clusters throughout the space. In the center of each cluster are small, wooden coffee tables with an array of different magazines spread out neatly upon them.

I sit waiting in silence for what feels like hours, though I know it must have only been forty-five minutes. Finally, a familiar voice breaks through the silence from across the room.

"James," starts Sheriff Burke as he speed walks toward me. "I came as quickly as I could. What happened?"

I look at Sheriff Burke and am surprised to see him out of uniform. I've only seen him out of uniform one other time in my life and it was at our downtown harvest festival last October. He's wearing a worn-out Atlanta Braves hat with a fish hook attached to the brim, a pair of nice denim jeans, and a plain, light blue shirt.

"I don't know," I answer. "We were painting the barn and all of a sudden, he started breathing heavy and fell down. The next thing I knew, he was unconscious."

Sheriff Burke slowly removes his hat and sits down on one of the green chairs to the right of me.

"Have you heard anything from the doctor yet?" he asks.

I twiddle my thumbs and try not to look directly at the Sheriff as I respond.

"I haven't heard anything in a while," I explain. "A nurse came out about thirty minutes ago and said that things could have been much worse. They said they'd come back out to deliver any new news."

"And how are you doing?" Sheriff Burke asks, placing his hat over his left kneecap.

This time, I turn and look at Sheriff Burke as I

answer.

"I'm scared," I answer. "If you would have told me a few months ago that Mr. Peterson would turn out to be one of my closest friends, I wouldn't have believed you. But the fact is, even when everything else in my life has felt unstable, his friendship has been consistent."

Sheriff Burke offers a subtle smile and crosses his arms across his chest.

"Well," he starts. "That's the way Chip Peterson is, and the way he always has been."

"I'll tell you this, James," he says, putting a hand on my shoulder. "I'm sure the feeling goes both ways. If you feel that way about Mr. Peterson, I guarantee that he considers you to be one of his closest friends as well."

I look away from Sheriff Burke, and stare aimlessly toward the long hallway of hospital rooms in front of us.

"Think about it, son," the Sheriff continues. "Since his wife passed on, Chip hasn't had many friends. No real family around here, either. The fact is, you've probably spent more time with him over the past few months than anyone else has spent with him in years."

It was sad to think that Mr. Peterson didn't have any real friends or family nearby.

Sheriff Burke sits up in his chair, places his hat back on his head, and crosses his right leg over the top of his left knee. He clears his throat and looks back toward me.

"So, how has the barn been coming along?" he asks, his arms crossed tightly.

"We're nearly finished," I say. "We've done all of the construction and now we're just painting. That's what we were doing today when —"

I find it hard to finish the sentence. My eyes drift away from Sheriff Burke and he nods his head, understanding.

"I'm not sure if Mr. Peterson mentioned this to you or not," Sheriff Burke starts. "But it was actually your grandfather, John, who helped him build his first barn."

"Yes," I say smiling. "He did mention that."

I turn toward Sheriff Burke.

"Did you know my grandpa?"

"Not as well as I know your Uncle Ira," he answers. "However, I did meet him years ago. He was a great man," Sheriff Burke says with a smile.

Sheriff Burke and I talk for a few more minutes before he tells me he needs to go. I sit alone for a while longer in the hospital waiting room, my eyes growing heavier and heavier. I decide to kill time by picking up and reading one of the outdated magazines laid out on the wooden coffee table in front of me. I don't read more than two or three paragraphs before my eyes begin to shut.

CHAPTER SIXTEEN

My eyes fly open at the sound of a soft, familiar voice.

"You can see him now, James."

It's the nurse I talked to earlier.

"Great," I say, still half asleep. I look down to see the magazine I was reading, still opened across my chest. I fold it closed and set it with the others on the wooden coffee table.

I follow the nurse out of the hospital waiting room and down a series of hallways. The hospital itself smells like cleaning products, though as we continue walking down the hall, the smell of chemicals is replaced by other, more foul odors. The lights in the hallway are bright and fluorescent and the door to every room we pass looks identical to the one that came before it, with the exception of a unique, plastic room number placed to the left of each door frame.

"Here we are," the nurse says. "Room 203."

She turns the metal doorknob and pushes the narrow, wooden door slowly open. As we enter the room, we hear a low volume conversation coming from inside.

"Dr. Hudson is just finishing up," the nurse whispers. "You're welcome to wait right here until he's finished."

"That's alright," says the man inside, talking to Mr. Peterson. "I'm finished now. Come on in."

The man walks toward us and extends a hand in my direction.

"I'm Dr. Hudson," he says with a wide, toothy smile. "And you must be James."

Dr. Hudson looks exactly as you would expect a doctor to look. He's wearing a long, white, lab coat, with a blue collared shirt underneath. Around his neck is a blue and white striped tie. On the left side of his coat is a small, silver pin that reads "Devon Hudson, M.D." The contrast of Dr. Hudson's dark skin makes his white coat seem even more white than it actually is.

"Well, your friend here gave us quite the scare," Dr. Hudson starts. "But he seems to be doing much better now. Well, feel free to visit for as long as you'd like, James. It's great to meet you."

The doctor turns to smile once more at Mr. Peterson before leaving the room.

While most of the hospital looks old and outdated, Mr. Peterson's room seems newly renovated and modern. A light blue wallpaper lines the walls of the room, contrasted nicely by the dark laminate flooring. Even though most of the room's light fixtures are off, the room is still plenty bright, rays of light flooding in from the window embedded along the room's far wall. I hear a steady beeping sound coming from the center of the room. The sound comes from a large, white machine standing tall near the slightly inclined bed in the center of the room.

Mr. Peterson looks tired. He lays on the bed with one hand rested motionless on his chest and his other arm tucked tightly into his side. Though his face is more pale than usual, and his eyes look much more tired, he still manages to keep a gentle smile on his face.

"I thought you were going to die," I finally manage to say, walking over to the visitor's chair on the right side of the hospital bed.

Mr. Peterson's smile disappears slowly and he manages to let out a subtle sigh.

"I suppose it wasn't my time to go quite yet," he says, almost reluctantly. "But I'll tell you this," he starts. "Whenever it is my time, I'll be ready."

I sit quietly in the stiff, wooden chair, my body hunched over and my elbows resting against my knees.

"You aren't afraid of dying?" I ask, amazed at Mr. Peterson's claim.

Mr. Peterson takes another big breath, closes his eyes and shakes his head slowly from left to right.

"Not one bit," he answers.

"Why not?" I ask.

"Well, James," he starts. "I've lived a long, full life. And I've done a lot in the years that I've been on this Earth. But that's not why I'm not afraid to die."

"Then what is it?" I ask.

"Do you remember what Pastor Chris was talking about on Sunday? About having faith in Jesus?"

"Yes," I answer, this time taking my eyes off Mr. Peterson and locking my sight on the dark brown laminate flooring.

"God created me for a purpose. There was a reason I was placed here on this Earth. But it was never intended to last forever. I lived my life the best way I knew how, James. I only wish I would have known the truth about God and Jesus sooner. But what I *can* tell you is that I have faith in Him. And that faith — that's why I'm not afraid. I have faith that God sent Jesus to Earth so that I could have the chance to have my sins forgiven. And because of that, and because I accepted Jesus into my life, I know that I'm no longer distant from God. By forgiving me of all the things I've done wrong, Jesus bridged the gap between God and me. I have faith in that. And I have hope for the future. A future life that starts when this one ends. A life that will last forever, with Jesus. With God. In Heaven. And I don't know when that next part of my life will start. But whenever God says it's my time, I'll be ready."

I look back at Mr. Peterson's tired face.

"I guess it's hard to be afraid of dying when you know

you have something like that to look forward to," I say.

Mr. Peterson shoots a quick smile in my direction.

"Can I ask you something?" I ask quietly.

"Anything," he answers.

"I got in a fight with Uncle Ira and Aunt Terry. We were talking about God and all this Christian stuff, and they don't believe any of it. And, well —"

I pause, trying to think how to word the rest of my question.

"Yes?" Mr. Peterson asks, looking straight at me.

"Well," I start. "If you think God exists, and Uncle Ira and Aunt Terry don't... someone has to be wrong. Right?"

Mr. Peterson is quiet for a moment. He takes his eyes off me and looks up as though he were searching for the answer to the question on the white ceiling above us.

"This is the difference, James," Mr. Peterson begins. "If I'm wrong, I've lost nothing. If they're wrong, they've lost everything."

Chills run down my spine as Mr. Peterson answers my question. I had never thought of it that way before.

Mr. Peterson and I both grow quiet. The only noise in the room is the constant beeping from the white machine to my right. The silence is broken by the sound of Mr. Peterson lifting his arm to reach for the tissue box on the table to his right. As Mr. Peterson brings a white tissue up to his nose, I notice for the first time that his eyes are slightly red and brimming with water.

"So," Mr. Peterson begins, changing the subject. "I

was thinking that you and I could finish up painting the barn in a few days when they let me out of here."

I shoot a smile toward Mr. Peterson.

"Sounds like a plan to me," I answer.

CHAPTER SEVENTEEN

I partly feel bad for lying to Mr. Peterson. I told him that I would wait for him to get out of the hospital so that we could finish painting the barn together. However, I thought it would be a nice surprise for him to be able to come home and see the barn completely finished. I haven't had to work alone, either. For the past couple of days, while Mr. Peterson has been in the hospital, I've had Scott and Sam helping me paint. They don't work with their hands very often (neither did I before this summer) and so they paint more slowly and with less precision than I do. But it's better than trying to finish the entire building by myself.

Every evening around four thirty or so, the twins and I stop painting for the day, and I go visit Mr. Peterson at the hospital. Yesterday, I told him more about the fight that I had with Uncle Ira and Aunt Terry. He told me I should call them and apologize for the things I said and the way I acted.

"You'll never know when it will be the last time you'll see them," he cautioned me. "None of us are promised tomorrow."

I went home and apologized as soon as I left the hospital that day.

I feel as though I've learned more about Mr. Peterson over the past couple of days than I have all summer. Each evening, I sit by his hospital bed and he and I talk for hours. Sometimes we talk about the barn, or fishing, or the "good ole' days" as he calls them. But no matter what we talk about, it's just nice being with him. Yesterday, he told me more about his wife, Allison. I wasn't surprised to find out that he keeps a small photo of her in his wallet.

"She was the love of my life for my entire life," Mr. Peterson told me, holding the wrinkled and worn-out photo in his shaky hands.

Today is a hot day, the same as nearly every day this summer. The twins and I plan to finish painting the barn this afternoon. We're down to the last patch of unpainted wood.

"I feel like I'm about to die in this heat," Scott says, complaining as usual.

"Well, suck it up," teases his brother. "Just imagine how you'd feel if you were James and had to build this thing from scratch *and* paint it."

Sam and I both laugh but Scott's frown doesn't budge.

"I'll tell you what," Sam starts. "If you boys keep painting and finish this up, I'll drive down to Edmund's and grab us all some Gatorade."

"Deal!" Scott and I both say in unison.

Sam sets his paint roller down and jogs off in the direction of the Ford Explorer.

Scott and I continue rolling fresh, red paint onto the bare wood of the barn as we hear gravel gently crackle under Sam's tires.

"I know I've already said this," Scott starts, holding the paint roller in one hand and placing his other hand on his hip. "But I really *am* sorry for everything."

I chuckle lightly.

"Scott, we've already been over this. I'm not upset. We're good. That's what friends do — forgive one another."

"I know, I know," he starts. "It's just... I can't believe you had to build this entire barn on your own without our help. I didn't realize it was going to be this big. Being here now makes me realize how big of a jerk I really was."

"Well, first of all, I didn't build it alone," I answer. "And secondly, you're right. You were a jerk."

A shoot a smile in Scott's direction, which he matches with a smile of his own.

Not more than five minutes after setting our brushes down and admiring our completed work, we hear the Explorer pulling back onto the Peterson property. Sam climbs out of the SUV with two unopened Gatorade bottles in one hand and one that's nearly empty in the either.

"Here you go, boys!" Sam shouts, throwing each of us a cold bottle.

The coolness of the bottle feels refreshing against the skin of my hands. Before taking a sip, I raise the bottle to my forehead, pressing it against my sunburnt skin.

"So, what now?" Sam asks, taking a final sip of his Gatorade. The three of us sit down on a shady patch of grass near the far side of the barn.

"Nothing," I say. "That's it."

I can't help but stare in awe at the freshly painted barn in front of us.

"It's hard to believe that a few months ago, there was nothing but ash and rubble here," I say, taking a long swig from the bottle in my right hand. "Now it's just as good as the old barn."

"It's better," Sam says.

The three of us sit together and talk for about an hour, occasionally taking a sip from our Gatorade bottles. We begin standing up when we hear a sound we haven't heard in a long time — the sound of thunder.

"Is that what I think it is?" Scott asks.

We all smile as we notice dark clouds forming in the sky above us.

"We'd better get out of here before we get soaked!" I say, quickly moving our paint brushes and paint cans inside the barn.

The twins and I jog toward our vehicles. It hasn't begun raining yet, but it seems as though it may start any minute.

"Are y'all heading to the house?" I ask, opening the door to the Camry.

"Yeah, we are. Where are you headed?" Sam asks in return.

"Take a guess," I say with a smile.

Sam smiles in my direction.

"Tell him we said hey."

CHAPTER EIGHTEEN

The sky is dark with rain clouds as I pull into the nearly empty parking lot of Thomasville General Hospital. I park the Camry and walk toward the large, white overhang near the front entrance of the hospital. The automatic sliding doors swoosh open as I step inside the lobby. I look over to the worn out, green chair that I sat in on the very first day. Though it was only a handful of days ago, it feels as though it's been much longer. I walk up to the counter and smile at the receptionist behind the glass barricade.

"I'm here to visit Chip Peterson in Room 203," I say.

"Ok, no problem at all," the woman says with a smile.

She types something into her computer. After a brief pause, her face shows a quick look of confusion.

"Take a seat, please," she insists. "Dr. Hudson will be

with you shortly."

I turn around and begin walking toward the empty waiting room. Before sitting down, I hear a familiar voice come from behind me.

"James!" Dr. Hudson shouts, speed walking in my direction.

Dr. Hudson is still several yards away, walking toward me from one of the long hallways on the other side of the waiting room.

Normally, his white smile is wide and bright, but tonight it seems less friendly and more serious. I can tell that something is wrong.

"How is Mr. Peterson?" I ask, the smile on my own face slowly beginning to fade.

"James," he starts. "Why don't you and I sit down for a moment?"

"No," I protest. "I don't need to sit down. How is Mr. Peterson?"

Dr. Hudson takes a quick breath.

"James, I'm sorry," he says in a low, monotone voice. "About an hour ago, Mr. Peterson passed on."

The words ring through my ears in an echo. Passed on. I look away from Dr. Hudson and toward the long stretch of hallway behind him in the direction of Room 203.

"No," I say, turning away, walking quickly toward the hallway.

"James, come back!" Dr. Hudson shouts behind me. "He won't be there!"

I can tell by the sound of jogging footsteps that he's following after me. My speed walk turns into a jog, and then into a sprint. I round the end of the first stretch of hallway, greeted again by the familiar stench of cleaning products and chemicals. Within a few seconds, I finally make it to the outside of Room 203. My heart sinks as I swing the door open. The room itself looks the same as it did yesterday, with the exception of a faint, sunken impression in the mattress where Mr. Peterson had once been.

"It was a surprise to us all," I hear Dr. Hudson say as he finally catches up to me. "Chip recovered from his heart attack at a record rate. He was a very healthy man. Strong. But he was getting up in years, and I suppose it was just his time."

I feel more tears begin to well up in the back of my eyes, though this time I try to repress them.

"His time," I repeat softly.

I remember what Mr. Peterson had said about not being afraid of death — about looking forward to "his time."

"I'm sorry James," Dr. Hudson says, gently placing his right hand on my left shoulder. "It's never easy losing someone you care about."

For the first time in the last several minutes, my smile resurfaces, only slightly.

"Thank you," I answer. "I think he was ready to go."

Dr. Hudson and I begin walking back to the hospital

lobby. We make our way down the long stretch of hallway, but before reaching the quiet waiting room, he stops me, pulling something out of his coat pocket. It's a crisp, white envelope with a name written across the front in blue ink — my name.

"A few days ago, Chip asked me to give this to you in case he passed," Dr. Hudson explains, handing me the envelope. "I didn't really think I'd be handing it to you, as he was doing so well. But I'm keeping my promise to pass it along."

"Thank you," I say softly.

I turn around and continue walking down the hallway toward the empty hospital lobby, tearing open the envelope's seal along the way.

"Have a nice night," I say in the direction of the receptionist as I continue walking toward the hospital's automatic, sliding glass doors.

The outside air is cooler than it was when I first entered the building only minutes ago. It hasn't begun raining yet, but the night sky is filled with black rain clouds. As I continue walking toward the Camry, I hear a low growl of thunder.

I peer inside the opened envelope in my hands, only to find a white piece of paper, folded in thirds. I slowly unfold it to find a handwritten note, written in blue ink:

James,

If you're reading this, it means that my time has come. Please don't feel sorry for me. If anything, you should be jealous of me! My old, frail body is gone. My pains and aching joints are behind me. I've told you this before, but I've longed for this day. If my life was a race, today marks the day I finally cross the finish line. And just like any race, this life of mine has had obstacles and barriers and challenges. But it's also offered wonderful sights and incredible memories. Two things matter most when you're running a race: why you run and who you run with. And I've been lucky enough to have many great running partners throughout my life. My dear Allison, your grandfather, and more recently, you.

Another growl of thunder echoes through the sky and I can just make out Mr. Peterson's handwriting from the warm glow of the parking lot's light posts. I lean against the metal hood of the Camry as I continue reading the letter.

When we began working together on the new barn, I thought that I might have a thing or two to teach you, not only about building a barn, but about life. However, nothing could have prepared me for how much I would end up learning from you. From the bottom of my heart, I want to say thank you. Thank you for your kindness. For your honesty. For your friendship. Your grandfather, John, would be so proud of the man that you've become. I know I am.

Your friend,
Chip

P.S. I hope to see you again soon.

Water continues building up behind my eyes, so much so that a few drops of tears fall onto the white paper in my hands. I stare for a few more seconds at Mr. Peterson's signature at the bottom of the letter before gently refolding the paper and placing it inside the envelope.

I slowly drop to the pavement of the parking space beside the Camry, my knees resting against the surprisingly cool concrete. I lift my hands from my side and slowly clasp them together in front of me.

"God," I start, tears still falling from my eyes to the pavement beneath me. "I don't know how to talk to you. And before today, I wasn't even sure that you existed. But now I know you do. I don't know why you'd want me, but if you do, then I'm yours. I know I've ignored you for my entire life. I've said terrible things about you. I've denied your existence. I've made fun of others who do believe in you. And I'm sorry. I'm sorry for the things that I've said. For the things I've done. For the way I've lived. I know now that you sent your son to Earth to die so that I could live and have eternal life. And if you were able to save my grandpa and Mr. Peterson, then please Jesus, save me, too."

My prayer is interrupted by a heavy sheet of rain

117

suddenly falling from the sky. I look up to watch as the small beads of water fall quickly toward the earth. It's been so many months since I've heard the sound of rainfall and the coolness of the water feels refreshing against my sunburnt skin. I would normally hustle to escape the rainfall and climb quickly into the Camry, but I find myself in no rush. I smile as I sit down on the cool pavement, leaning my back against the wet, metal door of the Camry. I can't describe the way I feel. I should feel sad, or mad, or upset that Mr. Peterson is gone. But I don't. I feel light. And full of a feeling that I haven't felt in a long time — hope.

As I slowly stand up and open the front driver's side door of the Camry, sheets of rain still falling from the sky, I think about both Mr. Peterson and my grandpa and how neither of them were able to live long enough to see me become a Christian. I almost pray another prayer asking God to somehow let them both know, but I don't. Something tells me I don't have to.

CHAPTER NINETEEN

The funeral starts today at ten o'clock. I was originally going to ride with Uncle Ira and Aunt Terry but decided to drive alone instead.

"Are you sure you don't want to ride together, Champ?" Uncle Ira asks, still fiddling with his jet-black tie.

"I'm sure," I answer. "But I'll still come by afterward for lunch. I just think a drive alone would be nice — to clear my head."

Uncle Ira shoots a quick smile at me, followed by a sigh of frustration at his tie.

"Do you mind giving me a hand?" he laughs, finally giving up.

"Of course," I answer.

As I undo his tie knot to start over from scratch, I

119

realize that I've never seen Uncle Ira wear a tie before — or any other dress clothes for that matter.

"There you go," I say, finishing up the knot, pulling it tighter around his neck. "You look great."

"You both do," says Aunt Terry, strutting down the living room's wooden staircase. Even though Aunt Terry gets dressed up more often than Uncle Ira, today she really pulled out all the stops. Her normally straight brown hair now falls against her shoulders in waves and she's wearing a jet-black dress that falls just below her knees.

"Well, you're a sight for sore eyes," Uncle Ira says, making his way over to Aunt Terry for a hug and a kiss on the cheek.

I give them both a quick hug and walk out the front door toward the Camry.

While today marks one week since Mr. Peterson's death, it also marks one week since I became a Christian. After visiting North Pike Baptist again a couple of days ago, I realized I still have a lot to learn about Christianity. I still don't know any of the songs or which part of the Bible each of the books are in, but that's ok. I'll get the hang of it all over time. After the church service last Sunday, I had a long talk with Pastor Chris, and he told me that being a Christian doesn't suddenly make you a perfect person or even take away the fact that you're a sinful person. It just means that your sins are covered and forgiven by Christ's blood. I also learned that being a Christian is a journey. It's a continual process of becoming more and more like Jesus.

Pastor Chris calls that sanctification.

I slowly pull the Camry onto the long, winding gravel road of the cemetery. I've only ever been to one other funeral service before. It was for one of Uncle Ira's close friends who suddenly passed. I was only nine at the time and didn't fully understand everything that was happening. The sign at the cemetery's entrance is the same as it was all those years ago. It's a large wooden sign painted green which reads "Laurel Hill Cemetery" in a thick white paint. The sign itself is fastened to a white lattice which stands tall directly behind it. On both sides of the sign are large, green bushes, planted in a dark brown mulch.

After driving only a moment, I can already tell that it will be difficult to find somewhere to park as lines of cars fill both sides of the narrow road, bumper to bumper. I see an opening three cars ahead and decide to parallel park there.

It's been raining nearly all week, but not today. The weather today is gorgeous — not a cloud in the sky, though not too hot either.

I step out of my car and start walking toward the funeral service area. Up ahead, I can see a large crowd of people, dressed in all black and a white canopy tent providing shade. I'm halfway to the tent when I hear a few familiar voices behind me.

"James," the voices whisper softly in unison behind me.

It's Scott and Sam. I slow down and let the twins

catch up so that we can all walk together the rest of the way. By the time we get to the white tent, we see several rows of white, wooden chairs pointed in the direction of a large wooden casket. We notice others beginning to find seats and decide to find a set of seats ourselves in one of the middle rows. I save a couple of seats for Uncle Ira and Aunt Terry, who I see walking in our direction a few dozen yards away.

I watch as Pastor Chris makes his way in front of the rows of chairs, standing between the wooden casket and a large photograph of Mr. Peterson.

"We are gathered here today," starts Pastor Chris. "To say farewell to Charles Bennett Peterson, and to commit him into the hands of God. As I look out at this congregation of faces, it's evident to me just how much of an impact Chip Peterson had on this town and on all of us here. For any of you in the congregation today that had a chance to truly get to know him, you know that Chip Peterson was a doer. He liked to get things done, but not at the expense of low-quality work. No, Chip Peterson got things done, but always with a dedication to excellence, a high-quality work ethic, and an attitude of gratitude."

I take my eyes off Pastor Chris for a brief moment and quickly scan the isles of chairs to my right and left. I don't recognize many of the people in the congregation, but every five or six seats, I see someone who looks familiar.

"I'm standing in front of you today because I was Chip Peterson's pastor," Pastor Chris continues. "But more importantly, I was his friend. And he was a friend of mine, too.

The week of his passing, I visited Chip at the hospital nearly every day. I think he knew that his time was slowly approaching and so he and I eventually got on the topic of what I would share at his funeral if his time *were* to come."

Pastor Chris takes a brief pause, directing his gaze away from the congregation and into the direction of the brown, wooden casket to his left.

"I asked him what I should say," he starts again. "And he told me to simply share about the friend that we both had in common, our Lord and Savior, Jesus Christ. You see, Chip was a great friend. Not only to me, but likely to every person here today. And there are three things that great friends always do. First, they tell you the truth, even when it's hard. Second, they love you unconditionally, no matter what you do or say to them. And third, they choose to forgive you, even when you've done something you may consider unforgivable. Chip lived that way and was that kind of a friend to everyone he knew. When I asked him how he became such a good friend, he told me that he was simply trying to be more like the best friend he's ever known — Jesus."

The message continued for several more minutes, followed by a hymn and a long prayer. Toward the end of the service, I looked over at Uncle Ira and Aunt Terry. I couldn't tell what they thought about the message. They seemed to have subtle smiles on their faces instead of the frowns and looks of dismissal that I was expecting, but that could have just been due to the fact that we were in a public setting.

As the service ends, everyone stands up, gathers their things, and begins making their way to their vehicles. I say goodbye to the twins and watch as more and more people leave the cemetery. I think Uncle Ira and Aunt Terry can tell that I'm not quite ready to leave yet.

"We'll see you at the house for lunch, right?" Aunt Terry asks, a sweet and delicate smile spread across her lips.

"Of course," I answer, returning her smile with my own. "I just want to stay for a few more minutes."

After another twenty-five minutes, the cemetery's narrow roads, once lined with vehicles, are now nearly empty. I'm the last one at Mr. Peterson's grave site, with the exception of a couple of men who seem to work for the cemetery. They continue folding up the white, wooden chairs, loading them onto the back of a large, black pickup truck.

The casket is now underground and is covered with a fresh patch of dirt. In front of the dirt is Mr. Peterson's tombstone. It's a light gray color and has a beautiful glossy shine.

"Thank you," I whisper in the direction of the stone. "Thank you for everything."

I look over my shoulder casually, making sure that neither of the two men are looking in my direction. I reach my hand into my left pocket and pull out Mr. Peterson's old, wooden pocketknife. I hold it in my hands for a brief moment, taking time to open and close it one last time before setting it gently on the tombstone in front of me.

I get up, brush the dirt from the knees of my pants and start walking in the direction of the Camry. I'm almost there when I notice another car parked directly behind mine. It's a black, shiny BMW with dark, tinted windows. Before I reach my car, the BMW's front door swings open and a man steps out of the car.

"James Connor?" the man asks, looking directly at me.

"Yes? I'm James Connor," I answer.

"My name is Kenneth Thompson," the man explains. "I was Mr. Peterson's lawyer."

As I take a few more steps in the direction of Mr. Thompson, I notice that he's carrying a black briefcase in his hands, matching his black, pinstripe suit. Mr. Thompson is an older man, perhaps in his late sixties. He has gray hair, a large, droopy nose, and dark circles under his eyes which are a stark contrast to the paleness of his skin.

"Do you have a moment to talk?" he asks, fidgeting with the briefcase in his right hand.

"Sure," I answer, a confused look on my face.

Mr. Thompson hoists the black briefcase onto the trunk of the BMW and fiddles with the numbers on the briefcase's combination lock.

"Chip visited my office a few weeks before he passed," Mr. Thompson explains, lifting the leather lid of the briefcase. "He told me that he wanted to make some changes to his last will and testament. You see, since Allison passed on, he hasn't had any family in the area — in fact, I'm not sure that he really has any at all to be honest. In any case, Chip asked that all material assets be passed down to you."

I'm stunned. I hadn't cried once yet today, but now feel tears beginning to well up behind my eyes. I take my eyes off Mr. Thompson and look into the distance, in the direction of Mr. Peterson's tombstone.

"Now," Mr. Thompson continues. "Chip didn't have much in savings, so most of what's left is in the form of material possessions such as his home, his barn, and his truck. I've already started the paperwork, and there are just a few forms for you to look over and sign to make everything official."

Mr. Thompson hands me a stack of papers, along with a metal ballpoint pen.

"I'm sorry for your loss, by the way," Mr. Thompson says. "You and Chip must have been very close."

My eyes drift once more into the distance and then back to Mr. Thompson.

"He was family," I answer.

CHAPTER TWENTY

It's hard to believe that it's already been ten years since that summer. Sometimes, it feels as though it's only been a year or two and other times it feels as though it was all something that happened an entire lifetime ago. It's funny how time works that way.

I finish ringing up another customer at the long, wooden checkout counter near the front of the store. It took a couple of years to figure out what to use the barn for. At first, we were using it as a personal storage building. That is until Laura, my wife, suggested that we open a country store and use the barn as a showroom. We sell just about everything in the store. Hand crafted wooden furniture, books, leather journals, novelty candies — we even have a rusty, dinged up drink machine outside that sells sodas for fifty cents. My life changed a lot after the fire. I became someone I never thought I could become. I learned that I had passions and talents and abilities that were hiding, dormant inside of me for the first half of my life. There's something about fire that is healing. It can burn down an entire building so that there's nothing left of it but ash and rubble. But more than that, it creates an opportunity. An opportunity to start again — to rebuild.

"Thank you for shopping at Peterson's," I say, giving Mr. Walker a smile as I hand him his change from the cash register in front of me. "Don't forget to make a s'more on your way out. We have a little bonfire lit out there and plenty of cold drinks!"

"Will do! Thanks, again, James," he answers. "Have a great day and tell Laura we said hello."

I watch as Mr. Walker and his two daughters walk away from the counter and in the direction of the large, sliding barn door at the other end of the room. Just as they walk out, a gush of cool November air rushes in, followed by another customer, this time a teenage boy carrying a basketball.

"Can I help you find anything?" I ask, crossing my arms and smiling in the direction of the boy.

"No thanks," he answers, bouncing the basketball a few times against the wooden floor of the store. "Just looking around."

"Feel free to look around but don't bounce your basketball inside the store."

The boy shrugs his shoulders, places the ball under his arm, and walks down the aisle closest to the entrance of the store.

I look through the window to the left of the checkout counter at the bonfire happening outside. We've been lighting the fire pit each Friday in November for the past two years as a way of attracting more business. It usually does the trick, too. Tonight, there are ten or eleven people gathered together outside, enjoying the warmth of the fire, listening to music, and sipping on RC Cola's from our fifty-cent drink machine. I watch as the flames of the fire flicker back and forth, dancing together against the cool, crisp air.

Still peering through the window's glass, I watch as Ray Anderson's two boys, who appear to be making s'mores, fight over the last piece of chocolate. I grab a few packs of Starbursts from the candy shelf to the right of the cash register, throw on my coat, and walk outside toward the fire.

"Afternoon, Mr. Anderson," I say, nodding in his direction.

"Good afternoon, James," he answers back, extending his arm for a handshake.

"You know," I start. "We're a little overstocked on a few supplies here at the store and I was wondering if you'd mind if your boys here took a few packs of Starbursts off my hands. I hear they're pretty good on s'mores."

"I don't mind a bit," Mr. Anderson answers. "What

do you say boys?"

"Ewww!" the boys shout in unison. "Starbursts with s'mores?"

I chuckle lightly and hand the packs of candy over to the boys.

"Don't knock it till you've tried it," I answer with a smile.

I watch as the boys begin unwrapping the candy and then turn around to head back inside. I stop for a moment outside the door to look up and admire the large, old, rusty, Peterson Lumber sign hammered to the front of the barn. I had the twins help me hang the sign up a few weeks after Mr. Peterson passed and it's been hanging up ever since. The barn just seemed unfinished without it. Plus, it seems like a nice way to honor Mr. Peterson.

Just as I walk back through the sliding door, I hear a loud thud from the far side of the room, followed by the sound of a bouncing basketball. I quickly pick up the basketball as it rolls in my direction and jog over to see what happened. As I make my way around the last aisle of the store, I see that one of the five handcrafted rocking chairs that once sat on the top shelf, along the back wall of the store, is missing. It isn't until I round the corner completely that I find out why. Sitting with his knees against the wooden floor of the barn is the boy, holding the broken arm of the rocking chair in one hand and using his other hand to frantically run his fingers through his hair.

"What on Earth happened?" I ask, still holding the

basketball in my hands.

He doesn't look back at me at first, but eventually turns his head in my direction.

"I'm so sorry," he answers. "I didn't mean for anything to break. I was just playing around."

I start to feel anger build within me as I continue looking at the broken rocking chair, quickly calculating how much time it will take to repair it.

"Didn't I tell you not to play with this in here?" I ask loudly, holding the basketball out in front of me.

"I'm so sorry," the boy says again. "I can buy it. How much is it?"

"Check the price tag," I answer softly.

The boy lifts the white tag attached to one of the wooden dowels near the top of the chair.

"Two hundred dollars?!" he asks. "I can't afford that."

I watch as he sets the chair's wooden arm onto the floor in front of him, a fearful look on his face. I remember that feeling. The feeling that you've ruined something that belongs to someone else. The feeling that you can't afford to pay the price to fix it. It's a feeling of despair. A feeling of hopelessness.

"What's your name?" I ask.

"Ryan," he answers softly.

"Well, Ryan, what are your plans tomorrow afternoon?" I ask him, kneeling down beside him on the cool, wooden floor.

"On Saturday? Nothing really. Why?" he asks.

"Well, if you can't afford to buy it," I start. "You can help me rebuild it."

Ryan looks back at me, confused. He's quiet for a moment, looking first at the broken chair and then back at me.

"Okay," he says. "That's fair."

I smile, handing the basketball back to him.

"I hope you're good with a hammer, kid."

Originally from a small town in Georgia, Brandan Ritchey has always found value in the power of story. After having written dozens of unpublished stories, he makes his published debut with *After the Fire*. Brandan is an evangelical Christian and worked in full time ministry for several years before launching his own business, Brandan Ritchey Creative.

brandanritchey.com

Made in the USA
Columbia, SC
23 October 2022

69918396R00083